HORSE THIEVES!

"Hey, what's this?" Lisa asked. She pointed to a piece of paper stuck to the wooden beam above the door to Garnet's stall. "I don't remember seeing that there before."

Stevie gave her a boost and Lisa reached up, pulling the paper down. When she landed, she opened the page and scanned the words printed there in block letters. Then she gasped. "It's a ransom note. Garnet's been horsenapped!"

Carole took the paper and read it.

WE HAVE YOUR HORSE. IF YOU EVER WANT TO SEE IT AGAIN, GET $10,000 CASH AND WAIT FOR ANOTHER NOTE FROM US. DO NOT CALL THE POLICE OR IT'LL BE CURTAINS FOR THE NAG!

Also available:

THE SADDLE CLUB

HORSENAPPED

BONNIE BRYANT

A BANTAM BOOK®

NEW YORK · TORONTO · LONDON · SYDNEY · AUCKLAND

I would like to express my thanks to
Alexander L. Robinson, III, and to Katie Cooke,
who each, in a special way, helped to give the book flavor.

THE SADDLE CLUB: HORSENAPPED
A BANTAM BOOK 0 553 40437 7

First published in USA by Bantam Skylark Books
First publication in Great Britain

PRINTING HISTORY
Bantam edition published 1991
Reprinted 1992, 1993, 1994

With thanks to Suzanne's Riding School, Harrow Weald, for their help
in the preparation of the cover.

Bantam Books are published by Transworld Publishers Ltd,
61–63 Uxbridge Road, Ealing, London W5 5SA,
in Australia by Transworld Publishers (Australia) Pty Ltd,
15–25 Helles Avenue, Moorebank, NSW 2170,
and in New Zealand by Transworld Publishers (NZ) Ltd,
3 William Pickering Drive, Albany, Auckland.

Printed and bound in Great Britain by
Cox & Wyman Ltd, Reading, Berks.

For Judy Gitenstein,
who has always been horse crazy

"SOMEDAY, I'M GOING to be that good," Carole Hanson told her friends Stevie Lake and Lisa Atwood. The three girls were watching the performance of an adult rider at Pine Hollow Stables' combined-training event.

"Of course you will be," Lisa said.

"No she won't," Stevie said. "Carole's going to be better than that."

Carole smiled to herself. She was glad that Stevie and Lisa were her best friends, and she hoped they were both right. All three of the girls loved everything about horses. They considered themselves horse crazy and had formed The Saddle Club so they could ride together and talk about horses just about any time they wanted.

Carole was the most experienced rider of the three. She'd learned to ride at the various Marine Corps bases where she had lived with her father, a colonel, and her mother, up until her mother's death two years earlier. Riding and horses were everything to Carole. Although she hadn't decided what she would be when she grew up, she knew it would have to do with horses. She might be a rider, a breeder, a trainer, a vet—or maybe even all of them! Her dark eyes shone with excitement at the very thought.

Stevie had been riding for a few years, too, and was almost as good as Carole, though her impulsiveness and tendency toward mischief sometimes interfered with her progress as a rider. Those qualities also frequently got her into trouble with adults and other people who didn't always see situations exactly the way Stevie saw them. Sometimes even her best friends didn't see things the way she did, but they always knew that whatever Stevie's scheme was, and no matter how harebrained it might seem, it was almost guaranteed to be fun.

Lisa, though a year older than her friends, was the newest rider of the three. Their teacher, Max Regnery, said she had natural ability. That, along with hard work, allowed her to keep up with her friends. Lisa enjoyed hard work. She worked hard at school as well as at the stable, and although her mother would have preferred more ladylike skills, such as ballet and painting, Lisa was proud of her accomplishments.

"Look at the way she gets her horse to turn the corner," Carole said. "That's what Max always wants us to do."

Lisa watched. She always learned from Carole and she didn't want this to be an exception. The rider in the ring, performing dressage—the first of the three sections of the combined-training event—was showing how well the horse and rider worked together in intricate patterns of steps, gaits, and forms. Some people said this was boring to watch. To an experienced rider, it showed more (or less!) skill than the other components of the event, the cross-country and the stadium jumping.

All three girls were competing in the junior events on each day of the competition. Although the events were similar to the adult events, the requirements for the junior events had been devised by Max for his young riders and didn't always follow the specific international rules of combined training events. He'd promised the girls that the events would be tough, though, and Lisa was sure of that. She was equally sure they would be fun.

One of the things Max was doing differently was that he'd decided to award ribbons in each segment of the competition as well as an award for the best overall competitor. Lisa didn't expect to win any blue ribbons. After all, she was a relatively new rider. But she hoped she'd be able to get a second or third in something.

"Who's up next?" Stevie asked, interrupting Lisa's thoughts while she scanned the program.

"It's Mrs. McMurtry, but then comes Alicia Downing. She's really great," Lisa said.

"And she's really nice, too. Let's go wish her luck," Carole suggested.

"Okay," Stevie agreed. "But tell me. Who is it you're wishing luck to? Mrs. Downing or that gorgeous championship Thoroughbred horse of hers, Bodoni?"

"I plead the fifth," Carole said with a laugh. "Let's go."

The three of them left their seats and entered the large, dimly lit tent that had been set up to house the event horses temporarily.

"It's over this way," Stevie said, leading the way and looking over her shoulder. Before she knew it she ran smack into something quite large, quite human, and moving very fast.

"Oomph!" she said. She lost her balance and landed on the ground.

"Oh, golly, I'm sorry, Stevie," the large, fast-moving human object said. It was Donald, Pine Hollow's newest stablehand. He offered Stevie a hand and helped her back to her feet. "It's just that I've got so much to do. Mrs. McMurtry's screaming about a smudge on her boots and then I have to see about water for two of the horses and I'm sure Max told me to do something else, but I can't remember what it was and there are six other things that I've got written down, so if you'll excuse me . . ."

Before Stevie could excuse him, he was gone. Stevie

shook her head in irritation. "I know he's working hard and I should have been looking where I was going, but look at this. I got dirt all over my riding pants and *I* have to look good for the dressage test, too."

"It's okay, it's just a smudge," Lisa said. Then she picked something up. It was a pack of watermelon-flavored bubble gum Donald had dropped. "I hate this flavor," she said.

"I'll take it," Stevie said, pocketing the gum. "I'll chew any kind of bubble gum. Besides, he owes me for knocking me over. Now, what am I going to do with these dirty pants?"

"Let's go over to the bathroom in the stable and I'll help you get the dirt off, okay?"

"You don't need me to help with that, do you?" Carole asked. Lisa shook her head. "Good. I'll go see Bodoni. Meet you back in the stands."

Carole worked her way through the maze of aisles in the tent, looking for Bodoni's stall. She did love that horse. He was a coal-black stallion, a full brother to another horse she'd loved, named Cobalt.

When she arrived at Bodoni's stall, though, it was empty. All his tack was there, so he wasn't being exercised. The stall door had been left open and swung out into the hallway, where it could trip somebody or knock into a horse. That was very strange. No horse owner would ever do that because no horse owner would ever want anybody else to do that. Carole was sure something was wrong.

"Where's Bodoni?" she asked Donald as he dashed past her on the way to one of his many chores.

"Dropped out," Donald called back over his shoulder.

That was even stranger. Bodoni was almost guaranteed to take a ribbon. Why would he drop out? Even odder, why would someone take him away and leave all his tack behind? Carole sniffed trouble. She wanted to find Alicia Downing and ask her what was up.

The tent was filled with people, but most of them were strangers to Carole.

"Have you seen Alicia Downing?" she asked one of the trainers. The woman just shrugged her shoulders.

Carole realized then that if Bodoni was gone, Alicia would certainly be gone, too. She wondered if she might find Alicia still loading Bodoni into his trailer. Carole dashed along the crowded aisles heading for the parking lot and loading area. She wanted to know what was going on with one of her favorite horses. She just had to see Alicia.

She saw Alicia, all right. At least, she saw Alicia's station wagon and horse trailer, driving out of the parking lot.

Carole waved to Alicia, hoping she'd stop and Carole could find out what had happened, but Alicia didn't wave back. All Carole saw was Alicia leaning into the steering wheel intently, and when the driveway turned, she saw the rear of the trailer as it bounced along the rutted path.

It could be a hundred things, Carole realized, and it could be nothing at all, but it could be something . . .

Carole was confused. The vivid image of the bouncing trailer made her wince on Bodoni's behalf. It must have been very uncomfortable for the horse. Then it occurred to her that it might have been intentional. It was well known that a horse with colic sometimes got relief by being driven around in his trailer. Maybe Bodoni was sick. That would explain why Alicia had dropped out of the event and left Bodoni's tack at the stall.

Satisfied that she'd figured out the most likely explanation, Carole decided to go back to the stands to meet Lisa and Stevie. There were four more adult competitors, including the other likely ribbon winner, and she wanted to see them all. When the adult competition was finished, there would be a break before the junior dressage began.

She made her way past the tent and over to the ring. Before she got there, though, she ran into Lisa and Stevie.

"All done," Stevie said. "You missed the last rider."

"The last? What about Bill Feeney?"

"He scratched," Stevie told her.

"Scratched?"

7

"She means he dropped out, withdrew," Lisa explained.

"I know what it means. But why?" Carole asked. She was disappointed. He was the other rider most likely to take a ribbon. Like Alicia, Mr. Feeney rode a valuable Thoroughbred. His was a mare named Saturday's Child, called Sat. She was descended from a Kentucky Derby winner. Carole loved to watch Sat move. Her long legs were so graceful that she seemed to fly. But she wasn't going to see her today.

"They didn't say why. They just said Mr. Feeney had withdrawn. That's too bad for him, but it's also bad for us because that means we're on in exactly one half hour!" Stevie reminded Carole and Lisa.

A half hour wasn't a lot of time and there was an awful lot to do. All thoughts of Bodoni and Sat left Carole's mind. Every bit of her attention had to be turned to her own horse, Starlight.

The three girls reached the stable together and then split up. They were responsible for their own horses. Carole went straight to Starlight's stall. He looked wonderful. She'd spent an hour and a half grooming him that morning. His coat was sleek and shiny. His tail was braided. She'd tried braiding his mane, but it was such a pretty deep black when it hung loose that it seemed a shame to braid it. Carole could have sworn that Starlight was relieved when she unbraided the parts she'd braided. Somehow, it seemed too fussy for him.

She carried his tack from the tack room back to his stall and tacked him up. It was a job she did almost every day in almost exactly the same way. This day, however, it seemed different. Carole always cared that Starlight looked well-groomed and well-tended. Today, for the first time, somebody else—namely a judge—was going to care, too. She'd soaped and polished his saddle until it had a deep sheen. She examined it again as she put it on him and she couldn't find a single blemish. There was no question about it. She was ready.

She patted Starlight and checked her watch. She still had ten minutes. Was there anything else?

She thought about her friends. For all three of them, this was their first real competition. Would it make any difference to them that they were competing *against* one another?

Carole didn't think so. After all, they were best friends. Not one of them would think of sacrificing their friendship for a ribbon. Still, Carole wondered. She knew she was going to try her best, and so would her friends. Would their best be good enough? Time would tell.

When Carole was sure there was nothing else to be done, she took a deep breath and opened Starlight's stall door. She held his reins in one hand and led him toward the stable exit nearest the schooling ring, where the competition was taking place. When she got to the door, she waited.

"Ready?" Stevie asked. She came up behind, leading the horse she rode, Topside.

"I think so," Carole said.

"Me, too," Lisa said, joining her friends at the door. Pepper followed her willingly.

"Then what are we waiting for?" Stevie asked.

Carole shrugged. She looked at Lisa. What were they waiting for, her look asked.

"This," Lisa said. She mounted Pepper and reached up by the edge of the door. The good-luck horseshoe was nailed to the wall there. Lisa touched it with her hand.

The horseshoe was one of Pine Hollow's oldest traditions. All riders touched it before they went out for a ride. No rider who'd done that had ever been seriously hurt.

Carole lifted herself into Starlight's saddle and touched the horseshoe as Lisa had. Stevie did the same.

"Now The Saddle Club is truly ready!" Stevie announced, leading the way to the warm-up ring where the horse would have a chance to loosen up and expend some energy.

"YOU'RE FIRST, STEVIE. Good luck!" Lisa said.

"You'll show them!" Carole encouraged her.

"Boy, I feel like I'm going into battle," Stevie said.

"Actually," Carole began, "dressage training was originally developed for battle horses by the Greeks. The theory was that if the horse and rider were perfectly trained to work together, then the horse would be better behaved in battle. That made it a lot easier for the soldier to fight. See, there's a reason for everything we do—"

Stevie began giggling. It was just like Carole to know some obscure fact, and to share it in detail—at just the most unlikely moment.

"I was just trying to help," Carole said, embarrassed.

"You did. You took my mind off how nervous I am. That helps. Thanks."

"Ready?" the starter asked Stevie. She nodded.

"Then here you go!"

Stevie heard the signal. It meant she and Topside had sixty seconds to enter the dressage ring. She felt relaxed, but she sensed a tenseness in Topside. She signaled him to walk by squeezing with her legs and shifting her weight forward a little. She made a large circle next to the entrance. No matter how nervous she felt, she had to hide it and make Topside feel as confident as possible. She breathed deeply and sat comfortably in the saddle. Topside relaxed as he walked in the lazy circle. Stevie knew he was ready.

The last word she heard as she entered the circle was "Smile!"

Stevie had been working on the dressage routine for weeks. She knew it by heart. She knew every turn. She and Topside were prepared for every lead change and step. The only trouble was that right then, she couldn't remember any of it.

Topside helped her out. He'd done the routine so many times before that it was almost automatic. He trotted to the center of the ring and stopped, facing the judges. Then Stevie remembered. The first thing she had to do was salute the judges. She'd practiced that enough, too. Dropping her right hand straight down, she nodded her head respectfully. The judges nodded back. That was done. Now what?

Once again, Topside helped her out. He walked toward the corner where her routine was to begin. The ring, a carefully measured twenty meters by forty meters, was marked, during practice, by one letter at each end and three letters on each side.

A

F   K

B   E

M   H

C

Each move Stevie was to make was described by the letters. She had entered the ring at A and trotted up the center to salute the judges at C. But now what?

Stevie took a deep breath. She was stalling for time, but it worked. When she breathed, she remembered that the routine started at M. She began trotting Topside toward the M corner and suddenly, it all came back to her, every move, every change, everything she and Topside had to do.

Topside was magnificent. Just as she had calmed him down before coming into the ring, he calmed her down as they began. Stevie felt his strong, supple body and it gave her courage.

Her first exercise was circles. She was to do them at the trot and canter. She began. The circles went just fine, although she posted for a few beats of the trot when she was supposed to do a sitting trot, but she didn't think anybody would notice. At least she hoped they wouldn't.

She then began her lead-changing exercises, which were basically figure eights. She remembered to sit for two beats to change diagonals at the trot when she was exactly at the cross of the eight. Topside handled the lead changes at the canter perfectly, but, Stevie told herself, that was because she had signaled him perfectly to do it.

The routine finished with a complicated serpentine walk, going from C to M to E to F to A to K and back again. Everything went fine until it was almost over. Then, when Stevie stopped in front of the judges' booth and turned to give her final salute, she realized she'd turned too far and she was facing away from them. That was a really awful thing to do. It was possible that a judge could miss the fact that she'd been posting when she ought to have been sitting, but there was no' way the judges could miss the fact that Stevie was saluting somebody else! She had to do something. Fast.

Then it came to her. She'd been working with Topside on turns, and although it wasn't part of her routine, she had the feeling she might just be able to pull it off. Using her inside rein to tell Topside where to turn and her out-side rein to tell him not to move forward, Stevie began. She put pressure on her inside leg, behind the girth. Her outside leg remained steady.

Without batting an eye, Topside performed a perfect turn on the forehand. His front legs remained where they were and his hind legs turned him a full 180 degrees. It was better than they'd ever practiced. Stevie grinned proudly. She saluted the judges. The judges smiled back and returned her salute. Stevie relaxed. It was over. All she had to do now was get out of the ring without falling off! She did.

"You were great!" Carole said. "I mean *great!*"

"I loved that turn. I didn't know you could do that!" Lisa said. "It was fabulous, and the judges thought so, too. I could see."

Stevie felt a little silly. After all, she hadn't meant to have to do the fancy turn. "It was sort of a mistake," she said.

"It certainly was!" somebody said coldly. The Saddle Club looked to see who was talking. It was Veronica di-Angelo. She was a snobby rich girl who owned her own purebred Arabian mare and who seemed to care more about how the horse looked than how well she rode her. "Showing off like that doesn't impress anybody. It's just a feeble attempt on your part to make everybody else look bad."

"That's not why I did it, Veronica," Stevie began, but then she saw that it was pointless to explain. Veronica saw everything exactly the way she wanted to see it. Since she'd decided Stevie had been showing off, trying to explain would only make it worse. "Well, maybe you're right," Stevie said. "I was showing off. But it wasn't to make you look bad. You look bad enough without my help." Stevie completed her remark with a smirk. She loved watching Veronica turn red with fury. It was very satisfying.

"Veronica, there's your signal," said the starter. "Ready?"

"You bet!" Veronica said. She yanked at Garnet's rein to turn her toward the gate and then kicked her to get her moving. Garnet was startled by the sudden actions and bolted into the ring. It was an inauspicious start.

The Saddle Club watched Veronica's whole performance, though it wasn't a pretty sight. Veronica was an experienced rider. She knew how to do everything in the test, but she got off on the wrong foot with Garnet and things just went from bad to worse. Instead of working *with* her horse, she was working *against* her. She yanked and kicked her way through all the movements. That made it look like a battle of wills in the ring, which was definitely *not* what dressage was about.

"I hate to see her treat that beautiful horse like that,"

Carole said. "Next thing you know, she'll be using her spurs on—oh, no! She did it!"

Stevie and Lisa couldn't believe their eyes. Veronica was jabbing her spurs into Garnet's flank. While it was true that many horses sometimes needed a reminder with spurs, Garnet wasn't the one who needed the reminder right then. It was Veronica.

She'd only gotten about two-thirds of the way through her program. Now, with that display of misbehavior, she burst into tears, wheeled Garnet around, and galloped her out of the ring. As soon as she was in the stabling area, she dismounted and handed the reins to an astonished Donald, interrupting him in the middle of blowing a bubble with his gum.

She stormed around to face Garnet, put her hands on her hips, and spoke to her harshly. "You *ruined* my program!" she said. "I don't ever want to see you again!" And she stomped off.

It was almost funny. Stevie giggled. Lisa tried harder and stifled it. Carole just felt sorry for Garnet. She was a good mare, just trying to do what Veronica asked. The problem was that Veronica had asked the impossible—mind reading. It was more than any horse could do. In fact, Carole told herself, reading Veronica's mind was more than any human could do!

"Carole, you're next," the starter said. "Ready?"

She was. So was Starlight. When she heard the signal, she entered the ring, to the calls of "Good luck" from her friends.

Carole and Starlight completed the program without difficulty, though Carole knew that they hadn't done as well as Stevie. Stevie, though she might sometimes be flaky and scatterbrained, was very good at dressage, better even than Carole. When the routine was over, Carole was satisfied she'd done the best she could. She was also satisfied that Stevie would have the best score in that event and that was just the way it should be. Carole patted Starlight proudly as they exited the ring. He was a young inexperienced horse who had done a pretty good job.

"Nice going, boy," she said. He nodded as if he'd understood her. Carole thought maybe he had.

Carole took Starlight back to his stall and untacked him right away when she was done. She had about ten minutes until Lisa was due to perform her program and she wanted to be there for that.

"I hate her!" Carole heard the unpleasant whine of Veronica diAngelo. Since Veronica hated a lot of people, Carole was curious to know who in particular she was berating at that time. "I don't ever want to see her again. That horse made me totally mess up on my dressage test!"

"Now, Veronica." Carole could hear Mr. diAngelo's

voice. Her father was trying to pacify her, but it wasn't working.

"I'm telling you to sell that horse to a dog food company. Today! That's all she's good for!"

"I'm sure you'll feel differently tomorrow, dear," her mother said.

"No, I won't. I don't ever want to ride her and nobody else should, either. She's awful. She didn't do a thing I told her!"

Carole cringed listening to Veronica's rantings. It was typical of her that she'd blame her horse for everything she herself had done wrong, but *dog food*?

"I hate her! I hate her!" Veronica continued fuming, insisting that her parents sell, "or better yet *give* her to a dog-food company!"

"Now, now, Veronica. There must be something we can do to make you feel better," Mr. diAngelo said.

"There *is*! Get that darned horse out of my sight!"

Her mother tried another approach. "Why don't we just take you home now and see if—say, didn't you say something about a sale at the mall? Would you like to stop there on our way home? That would make you feel better, wouldn't it?"

The whole thing sickened Carole. It was just typical of Veronica's parents to think they could buy their way out of one of Veronica's tantrums. The last thing Carole heard as she slipped out of Starlight's stall was Veronica informing her mother, once again, that the only thing that would make her feel better would be to destroy Garnet. Carole couldn't stand to listen to any more. Besides, it was almost time for Lisa's test.

She got to the gate of the ring just in time to wish Lisa good luck. Carole and Stevie practically held their breaths through all of Lisa's performance.

"Nice corners," Stevie said. Carole agreed.

"And look at the line of her arm and her reins. Almost perfectly straight."

"Almost, yes. That's good," Carole said. "She's really learned a lot for somebody who only began riding recently."

Apparently the audience agreed because when Lisa was done, there was a lot of clapping. The judges, too, looked pleased. Lisa, however, had a grimace on her face when she came back to her friends.

"I made so many mistakes!" she said to Carole and Stevie.

"Sure you did," Carole said philosophically. "But you also did an awful lot right. You did a good job out there. Next time, you'll do better. That's all."

"I guess you're right. But trotting on the wrong diagonal? I shouldn't have done that."

"No, you shouldn't," Stevie said. "But you handled the change of gaits perfectly. I'm sure the judges noticed that more. Come on. I'll help you untack Pepper. He deserves a treat and I know where we can find some carrots."

Stevie held the reins while Lisa dismounted. Then Lisa patted Pepper's neck and rubbed his cheek. He'd done everything she had asked of him and that was a lot.

"Good job, Pepper," she said. "I'll try to do better next time, and when I do, you will, too. Want some carrots now?" Pepper started for his stall without further prompting. "And Max says horses don't understand English!" Lisa joked, smiling at last.

Carole went with her friends, but watching Lisa hug Pepper reminded her that there was another horse that needed some consoling in the form of a carrot, and that was Garnet. Although the mare had also done everything her rider had asked, she'd gotten no thanks at all. When Stevie found the carrots Max had stowed in the refrigerator, Carole picked up a few extras for Garnet, whose stall was near Pepper's.

It wasn't easy to walk through the stable today because of all the competitors, plus parents and grandparents. Red O'Malley, Pine Hollow's chief stablehand, groomed one rider's horse while Donald led one horse to his stall and carried tack for another over his arm. The place was buzzing with activity.

The three girls were almost unaware of what was going on around them. It was always that way when they were talking about horses. The subject was dressage competition and the importance of dressage skills to all riding—not just for Greek military maneuvers—while they walked Pepper back to his stall. They were so involved in their conversation that Carole almost didn't notice that Garnet's stall was empty until she was standing in it, holding three carrots in her right hand.

"Garnet?" she said. Then she felt silly. It wasn't as if she could call her and she'd come out of hiding. There was no place for a full-grown Arabian mare to hide in a ten-by-ten-foot box stall.

"Where is she?" Carole asked, peering out over the wall to the stall, wondering if the mare might be cross-tied somewhere in the hall. "Did we pass her or something?"

Stevie was standing in the hall. She looked both ways. "No, not here. Where do you think she went?"

It wasn't as if the diAngelos would take Garnet home. This *was* her home. Then Veronica's words came echoing through Carole's head.

"Oh, no!" Carole said.

"What is it?" Stevie asked.

"Dog food!" Carole said, stepping out into the hallway.

"Huh?"

Carole explained. She hadn't had time to tell her friends about Veronica's tantrum. Besides, it hadn't seemed any different from any other tantrum Veronica had ever had, and she hadn't taken Veronica's demands

22

any more seriously than her parents had. But now, there wasn't any sign of Garnet. Had Carole underestimated Veronica's hold on her parents?

"Dog food? Give me a break!" Lisa said, emerging from Pepper's stall with his tack in her hands. "There must be another answer. Let's look in the stall and see if there are any clues."

"Sure, we can be horse detectives," Stevie said. "It's a puzzle and we'll solve it."

Skeptically, Carole returned to Garnet's stall. Stevie and Lisa were right behind her. At first, everything looked normal, just empty. The straw was pretty fresh, indicating that Garnet hadn't spent much time there since she'd been groomed. There was plenty of water in her bucket, confirming the same thing.

The words *dog food* kept running through Carole's head. They seemed to blank out all other thoughts.

"Hey, what's this?" Lisa asked. She pointed to a piece of paper stuck to the wooden beam above the door to the stall. "I don't remember seeing that there before."

Stevie gave her a boost and she reached up, pulling the paper down. It wasn't easy because it was stuck up there with chewing gum. When Lisa landed and took the remaining wad of sticky gum off the paper, she opened the page and scanned the words printed there in block letters.

"Oh, no," she said.

"Dog food?" Carole asked.

"No, worse," Lisa said. "It's a ransom note. Garnet's been horsenapped!"

Carole took the paper and read it herself.

"WE HAVE YOUR HORSE. IF YOU EVER WANT TO SEE IT AGAIN, GET $10,000 CASH AND WAIT FOR ANOTHER NOTE FROM US. DO NOT CALL THE POLICE OR IT'LL BE CURTAINS FOR THE NAG!"

"HORSENAPPED? YOU MUST be kidding!" Stevie said.

"I'm not kidding. That's what this says." Lisa handed her the note to read.

"Poor Garnet," Carole said.

"We've got to call the police," Lisa said sensibly.

"No way!" Carole told her. "These guys said not to. We can't endanger Garnet's life!"

"Then we'd better get this to Mr. diAngelo. It's a good thing he's so rich. He'll never even notice the ten thousand dollars is gone," Stevie said.

Carole's mind was racing and she didn't like any of the thoughts that were racing through it. "Wait a second," she said. "There's more to this than meets the eye. Much more, maybe. Don't go rushing off to tell anybody anything. First, we have to think."

"Well, if we're going to think, let's at least find some peace and quiet. This place is a zoo today," Stevie said.

"Okay," Carole agreed. "You two finish up the work on Pepper. I'll get us some sodas and I'll meet you at the hill above the paddock. Everybody's by the ring so we should have a little quiet. Five minutes, okay?"

"Okay," Stevie said. She and Lisa got right to work.

Carole had work to do, too. Her first step, as promised, was the cooler, where she picked up three sodas. Her second stop was the tented stabling area. She headed straight for Bodoni's empty stall and began to examine it carefully. The stalls had been created from walls of metal bars latched together. She entered the stall and looked back at the entry. The poles there reached to the top of the tent. Carole's eyes ran upward along the gray metal pole. And then they stopped. There, more than six feet above the ground, was a smear of something. Carole stood on her toes and reached up. Her fingers barely touched it, but there was no mistake. It was the remains of a small gob of chewing gum. Unless she was very mistaken, Alicia hadn't withdrawn from the competition because Bodoni was colicky. She'd withdrawn because he'd been horsenapped!

Carole's next job was to find where Bill Feeney's horse, Saturday's Child, was stalled before he'd withdrawn so mysteriously from the competition. She hadn't seen any signs from his stable. She could just wander around the tent, or she could—

"Oh, Donald!" she called to the stablehand as he raced past her. He slowed down. She jogged along with him. "Do you know where Saturday's Child is?"

"I'm in a real rush, Carole," he said. He began running even faster as if to prove it.

"I know. You don't have to do anything. Just tell me where the horse is."

"How should I know?" he asked. "All I heard is that his owner—"

"—*her* owner," Carole corrected him. Even in a terrible rush, she couldn't let him make a mistake like that. "Saturday's Child is a mare."

"Right. Anyway, she withdrew."

"I know. But where *was* she stabled?"

He slowed for a second and glanced around as if he was trying to orient himself. "Over there, I think," he said, pointing to the far corner of the tent. "I'm not sure, though."

Before Carole could ask him anything else, he dashed off. She headed in the direction he'd pointed. While it was true that there were over fifty horses entered in the competition, and more than thirty of them were housed in this tent, it seemed odd that a busy and conscientious stablehand like Donald couldn't remember where one was housed, especially a valuable Thoroughbred like Sat.

When Carole reached the section he'd pointed to, she found a stack of the temporary walls that had formed stalls. If there had been a stall here and if Sat had been in it, it was gone now. For a moment, she began to examine the pile of poles and walls, but realized soon it wasn't going to do her any good. She wasn't sure that this was where Sat's stall had been and if she *did* find a wad of gum, what would it tell her? People were forever parking gum in places they shouldn't. It wouldn't mean anything. Something stopped her eyes. It was the remains of a wad of gum stuck to a long pole. But, as she'd already told herself, it didn't mean anything. Probably.

Carole glanced at her watch and then did a pretty good imitation of Donald dashing. She arrived at the hill by the paddock, breathing hard.

"What happened to you?" Lisa asked. "We were afraid you might have been horsenapped."

"She means kidnapped," Stevie told Carole, who had already figured it out.

Carole handed each of her friends a can of soda, warned them not to open them right away because she'd been running so fast, and then sat down on the grass next to Lisa. Stevie opened her soda. It practically exploded, spurting a fine spray in the air.

"Ahhh, that feels great!" Stevie said.

Although Carole wasn't too enthusiastic about sticky stuff all over her riding clothes, she had to admit that

28

there was something to be said about cool soda on a hot day.

"Down to business, girls!" Lisa reminded her friends. She brought out the ransom note and laid it on the ground in front of her. "What exactly are we going to do to save Garnet?"

"Well, for one thing, I don't think it's just Garnet," Carole said. Both Lisa and Stevie looked at her in surprise. Carole told them about her suspicions.

"I had already decided that Alicia took Bodoni out in his trailer because he had colic, but then when Sat withdrew too, well, it seemed suspicious."

Then she told about the gum she'd found.

"You mean we're not dealing with a single incident, it's serial horsenapping? Or else it's a lot of single incidents with the same MO!" Stevie said.

"MO?" Lisa asked.

"*Modus operandi.* It's Latin for method of operation," Carole explained. "But what it really means is that Stevie's been watching too much television."

"Who cares what it's called. What's important here is that we nab the nappers!"

"Before they hurt the horses," Carole added.

"Wait a minute," Lisa said. "What's this about 'we'? Isn't this something the owners and the police should handle?"

"I've been thinking about that," Carole said.

"No way!" Stevie interjected. "Remember what the note said about calling the police."

"So, what about calling the diAngelos?" Lisa asked. "It certainly didn't say not to do that!"

"No, but you're not thinking" Stevie said. "If we call the diAngelos, or bring them the note, what are they going to do?"

"Have us arrested?" Lisa suggested. "It might look like we are in on it."

"Veronica may be that stupid, but her parents aren't," Stevie reasoned. "No, what they'll do is either call the police or pay the ransom."

"So?" Carole asked. She wanted to know what Stevie was driving at. This was beginning to get the feeling of one of Stevie's "schemes." Those were sometimes big trouble, and this one had trouble written all over it.

"Don't you see? If they call the police, then Garnet's a goner, and probably Bodoni and Sat, too—"

"*If* Bodoni and Sat were also horsenapped."

"Yeah, *if,* but it seems pretty certain to me. Anyway, calling the police is wrong."

"And what's wrong about paying the ransom, getting Garnet back, and *then* calling the police?" Lisa asked.

"Nothing," Stevie said. "That is, *if* they get Garnet back after they pay the ransom. Just because a crook makes a deal, it doesn't mean he's going to hold up his end of the bargain, does it?"

"What are you saying?" Carole asked.

"I'm saying that if we tell anybody about this, Garnet is in danger."

"But it's going to be a little hard to hide the fact that Garnet isn't in her stall," Lisa said sensibly.

"Oh, no, it won't be," Stevie said. "See, there's this event going on. Everybody's too busy worrying about himself to notice anybody else. Besides, Veronica's been disqualified because of walking out in the middle of her performance, so she won't be here and neither will her folks."

"Max," Carole said. "He's going to notice. So will Donald and Red. After all, they are the ones who take care of Garnet most of the time."

"I'm working on it," Stevie said. "I'll come up with something."

"It's going to have to be good," Carole said. "After all, Garnet's life is at stake."

"Aha! I've got it! We'll tell Max that the diAngelos took Garnet to stay in their field for a couple of days because they thought there was so much going on here it was upsetting her."

Carole scratched her head. It had possibilities, but she wasn't sure it would work. "Hmmm."

Lisa, the most logical of the three, took over. "Two things are wrong with that," she said. "In the first place, Max will call the diAngelos to make sure Garnet is okay and to be certain they're not upset with him."

"No way," Stevie said. "At least not until after the event is over."

"Maybe," Lisa conceded. "But when the event is over and Max does call them and finds out it's not true, he's going to say *we* told him that and we'll be in a lot of trouble, if not jail."

"So, then, maybe the thing to do is to let him *think* that's what they've done with Garnet and not exactly *tell* him."

"That's okay, up to a point," Lisa said. "And the point is the end of the event. The minute the dust settles on this three-day event, Max is going to be back to normal and he'll call. I agree with Stevie that telling may not get the best result for Garnet, but if we haven't gotten a better one by the end of the event, we're going to have to tell."

"If we haven't gotten a better result by then, we can pretend to discover the ransom note. How about that?" Stevie asked.

"This all sounds pretty cloak-and-dagger to me," Carole said.

"Yeah, but it's for the good of the horses, especially Garnet," Stevie reminded her.

"I hope those guys know what they're doing with the horses," Carole said. "I mean, those horses need really good care. I hate to think what would happen if the nappers got careless with the feed and grooming."

"Don't worry," Stevie said. "We'll figure out a way to find them and save them before anything bad could happen to them. We just have to think of a way to sneak up on them. I can see it now. We'll be on the front page of the newspaper, heck, every newspaper in the country!"

"Wait a minute! We don't want to sneak up on anybody!" Lisa interrupted Stevie's daydream. "We just want to figure out where the horses are and who did the napping, and then we want to let the police take over. We don't want to be heroines!"

Carole nodded agreement. "I don't know about you two, but the only thing that matters as far as I'm concerned is the safety of the horses."

Carole opened her soda can carefully. It didn't explode. As she took a sip, she looked down at the ring, where the last junior rider was completing his dressage test. Carole stood up.

"Time to go find Max and plant the idea that the diAngelos have Garnet."

"And then we'd better get out of here," Stevie said. "There's work to be done. I just got a great idea for a disguise, in case we need it. My dad has this old raincoat and a fake mustache . . ."

Lisa almost laughed. When Stevie got an idea for a scheme in her head, she sometimes got carried away. An old raincoat and a fake mustache definitely meant being carried away. But, after all, Stevie was probably joking. Lisa hoped she was.

One of the great things about The Saddle Club, as far as Lisa was concerned, was how different the three of them were. Stevie had her schemes; Carole was focused totally on the horses; and Lisa was logical. Their differences had always made them greater than the sum of their parts, but would it be enough this time?

"Hey, I just remembered something!" Stevie said, brushing dirt off her breeches. "My mother has this gigantic magnifying glass. We'll have lots of use for that!"

Carole's mind was on something else, as usual. "Maybe I should take out an ad in the paper with instructions to the horsenappers on how and when to feed those horses."

"Okay, first things first," Lisa said. But nobody was listening.

ACCORDING TO LISA, the first thing they had to do was find out if Bodoni and Sat had been horsenapped along with Garnet. Stevie was convinced it was true, based on what she referred to as "circumstantial evidence." Carole wasn't certain what circumstantial evidence was, but suspected it had to do with the gum. What it came down to was that Lisa assigned Carole the job of finding out for sure.

The next morning, the alarm next to Carole's head went off very early. It almost wasn't necessary, though. She'd been awake a lot of the night figuring out exactly how she was going to do what Lisa wanted her to do. Then, every time she actually started to drift off to sleep, she started worrying about the horsenappers taking proper care of the horses, and that made her wide-awake. She was glad when it was morning and she could at least stop worrying about one thing—sleeping.

The three girls were all staying at Stevie's house for the duration of the combined-training event because Stevie lived the closest to Pine Hollow Stables. Carole slipped out of bed without waking her friends. In the dim gray light of dawn, she put on her riding clothes and then, carrying her boots, crept downstairs to the kitchen. She drank a glass of milk and pulled on her boots. She and Starlight had some work to do and the sooner she started out, the better. Today was the cross-country riding part of the event. That meant Starlight would have *two* cross-country trips. The first one wouldn't count for a ribbon, but it might help make a difference to Garnet, Bodoni, and Sat.

Carole scribbled a note to her friends, saying she'd be back to Pine Hollow by midmorning. Then, she left the Lakes' house, closing the kitchen door behind her quietly.

ALTHOUGH CAROLE WASN'T always enthusiastic about getting up early, she was always happy she made the effort. There was something very special about stables and horses early in the morning. That was particularly true now, when early morning was the only time Pine

Hollow wasn't completely overrun by competitors, grooms, trainers, parents, and just plain spectators.

It only took a few minutes for Carole to tack up Starlight. He seemed as eager for an early-morning ride as Carole was. She led him to the door of the stable, mounted up, touched the good-luck horseshoe, and they were off.

Willow Creek, Virginia, wasn't a very large town. A lot of the people in and around town were involved with horses, and most of them knew one another. Both Alicia Downing and Mr. Feeney had property near Pine Hollow. It wouldn't take Carole long to visit them, particularly since she could take shortcuts across the fields behind Pine Hollow.

The air was still cool, giving little hint of the hot, humid day to follow. Dew hung on the grasses in the fields. It would evaporate as the morning warmed, lifting slowly above the field to meet the day. Everything smelled fresh and clean. Everything looked peaceful.

Starlight nodded his head, eager to get going.

Alicia's house was across three fields and a little uphill from Pine Hollow. The short ride was a good chance to let Starlight loosen up. Carole didn't want to tire him. He had a lot of work ahead of him with the cross-country ride later on, but a relaxed trip through an open field was something they could both enjoy.

Carole checked her watch. It was eight o'clock when she reached Alicia's house. She could hear a radio on in the kitchen, so somebody was up. Although Carole had been worrying all night about a plan, she wasn't like Stevie and hadn't come up with any clever way to do the detecting. Stevie had had lots of suggestions, but most of them involved clever and devious tactics that Carole had no faith in at all. So, Carole finally settled on the obvious. She decided to ask directly.

She tied Starlight's reins to Alicia's mailbox, walked up to the kitchen door, and knocked.

"Who is it?" came the startled response.

"Um, it's Carole Hanson, from Pine Hollow?" she began nervously. "I was just riding by this morning. I mean, I was exercising my horse because we're competing later on, and I thought I'd stop by because I missed seeing you on Bodoni yesterday and I was just, sort of wondering . . ."

Carole knew she was stumbling through her spiel. She sounded dumb and she couldn't help it.

"I'm really busy right now," Alicia said through the screen door.

"Well, I'm sorry to interrupt," Carole said. She wasn't going to be put off. "I just wanted to make sure Bodoni was all right. I mean, you left in such a hurry yesterday."

"He's fine," Alicia answered curtly. "This just isn't a good time—"

"Is he in the barn out back?" Carole asked, persisting.

Alicia seemed to pause. She definitely looked uncomfortable. "Of course he is," she said. "Where else would he be? I *really* can't talk to you now."

The door closed.

"Bye," Carole said politely to the air.

But she didn't mean it because she wasn't ready to leave. She returned to Starlight and mounted up. She rode behind the house as if she were going back through the field, but after she'd passed the barn and was out of sight of the house, she doubled back. It took only a quick look inside to confirm her suspicion: There was no sign of Bodoni.

"What are you looking for?" Alicia's voice came from a few feet behind her. She had followed Carole, making sure she'd gone, and now Carole had been caught red-handed snooping around the woman's barn.

Carole thought fast. "I just thought I could get a little water for Starlight," she stammered. She didn't fool Alicia, though.

"There's a trough in the field, Carole," Alicia said. "And you know it's there. You and your horse are welcome to the water. You are not welcome in my barn. I told you this wasn't a good time for a visit. Now, please, leave."

Alicia stood and watched while Carole mounted up

and rode away. There would be no doubling back this time, but there was no need to do it, anyway. Alicia hadn't exactly told her that Bodoni had been horse-napped, but it was clear that something was very wrong and that it had to do with Bodoni. Carole was even more convinced she'd been right.

Carole was pretty sure that if she spoke with Mr. Feeney, she'd get the same reaction she'd had from Alicia. She concluded, then, that there was no point in talking to him. She'd go right to the horse's mouth.

Mr. Feeney had a small stable to the side of his house. Carole approached it from the side away from the house. The stable was unlocked. She and Starlight stepped in. It was empty—just as she had expected. She had been in enough hot water for one day.

Carole checked her watch. It was time to get back to Pine Hollow. There was a lot of work to be done, not the least of which was the cross-country competition.

As Carole headed back over the fields to Pine Hollow, Max, Red, and Donald were working on the finishing touches for the junior course. The cross-country trail would take the riders in open areas as well as wooded ones. There were a lot of obstacles the riders and horses had to clear. It was a little bit like a hunting trail and Carole suspected it would turn out to be a lot of fun. Max saw her and waved. Red did, too. Donald regarded her quizzically. Carole thought maybe he was worried that she would overtire Starlight.

She leaned forward and patted Starlight's neck. He wasn't tired at all. He loved a brisk ride in the early morning. Just to prove it, he whipped his tail up brightly and lengthened his stride. He was ready.

STEVIE AIMED THE hose at Topside for a final rinse. She'd shampooed every inch of him so his coat would gleam for the afternoon competition. Now, satisfied, she turned off the water and tugged gently at his lead rope to move him from the bathing area. It was time to dry him and finish his grooming.

The horse didn't budge. "Come on, boy," Stevie said. He still didn't want to move. Stevie knew what the problem was. He loved being bathed and he didn't want it to stop. He was just like her little brother Michael. He never wanted to get out of the tub, either. The only way she'd ever been able to get him out was to tell him that Alex or Chad, her two other brothers, were playing with his Nintendo games. She had the funniest feeling that ploy wouldn't work with Topside.

"Yeah," she said to him. "You're always glad to share your Nintendo games, aren't you?"

Topside didn't answer. It was as if he had decided he wouldn't move or react to anything until he got more shower time.

"Okay, that's it!" she said in her most motherlike voice. "If you don't get out of the shower right this minute, there will be no dessert for you tonight!" She tugged at the lead rope as she spoke.

For some reason, Topside got the message. He followed Stevie to the area where she could dry him off. Stevie was relieved he'd obeyed, but she did wonder what, exactly, she was going to have to give him for dessert.

"He looks great!" Lisa said. She was in the hallway where her horse, Pepper, was cross-tied for his grooming.

"Thanks," Stevie said. "And Pepper looks ready for the Embassy Ball!"

Lisa nodded proudly. Pepper was a dappled gray. His coat didn't shine the way Topside's deep, rich brown did, but it certainly looked better when he was well curried and brushed.

"I was just wondering why horses are willing to stand still so long to be fussed over with grooming. Do you know?" Lisa asked.

"Sure. They love it," Stevie said. "They love the attention, and a lot of the stuff, like the bathing, brushing, and combing, just feels good. I don't think horses are too enthusiastic about having their feet picked, but a lot of them know that it feels better when it's done, so they put up with it."

That sounded reasonable to Lisa. Then something else occurred to her. "Well, if that's the case, how come we have to be careful on the trail not to let them get near a dirt or mud patch because they'll roll in it?"

"Hmmm," Stevie said thoughtfully. "Good question."

"Two answers," Carole said, joining her friends. She was leading Starlight back to his stall from her morning adventure. "In the first place, they do it to scratch or cool off. In the second place, they do it so they get very dirty so they have to be groomed all the more."

"Now, there's horse logic," Lisa said.

"And it makes complete sense," Stevie said.

"If you're a horse!" Lisa concluded.

"Excuse me! Excuse me, coming through!" It was Donald, pushing a wheelbarrow of fresh hay. The three girls and their horses were blocking the aisle. Donald would have to duck under their cross-ties to make it through the traffic jam. The girls didn't have a chance to move before he began threading a path around the horses, and he was gone before they could clear a way for him.

"What was that?" Lisa asked.

"A whirling dervish!" Stevie observed.

"Somebody who didn't know what he was doing," Carole added. "It was reckless to push that wheelbarrow right behind Topside. Donald hasn't been here long enough to know if Topside is a kicker or not."

Lisa looked down the aisle at the quickly disappearing Donald. Carole was right and it was puzzling. Everybody knew that horses had individual personalities. Some could be quite dangerous if you weren't careful. Donald hadn't been careful. He'd been lucky. Topside was a great horse, almost unflappable. But if Donald had pushed the wheelbarrow that close to Starlight's rear, he'd have stood a good chance of making an aerial exit from the stable!

She shared the thought with Stevie and Carole.

Stevie laughed. "Maybe that's how he seems to fly around here all the time, doing seventeen chores at once!"

"Then we're in good shape," Carole said. "All we have to do is two at a time."

"How's that?" Lisa asked.

"Well, first of all, we have to win blue ribbons; and second, we have to find some missing horses—three of them, to be exact!"

Stevie's eyes lit up with excitement. "Aha, the game's afoot!" she declared, borrowing a phrase from Sherlock Holmes. "I think we ought to have a Saddle Club meeting."

"Definitely," Carole agreed. "Let's finish our grooming and then get to the hayloft so I can tell you about my adventures this morning. Something tells me we shouldn't talk here."

"Aha," Stevie said. She spoke conspiratorially. "The stalls have ears!"

A FEW HOURS later, Lisa was ready for competition. At least she hoped she was. She'd spent the first part of the morning grooming Pepper, and the last part of it hearing about Carole's early-morning ride. At a time when she should have been able to focus solely on the competition, her mind was a total jumble of horse-related confusion.

The cross-country ride was a three-mile trail through fields and forest, up and down hills and over obstacles. The idea was to complete the course in a specified amount of time, negotiating all of the obstacles properly. It wasn't a race. In fact, taking too little time cost points. The rider had to maintain an even pace. Max had given all of the entrants a map of the course the day before and they'd all been allowed to walk it if they wanted. The Saddle Club had been so busy worrying about Garnet that they had only walked the course once.

Lisa was afraid that not covering the course a second time would hurt her chances, but a look at the map told her it probably wouldn't make any difference. She and Carole and Stevie had spent many hours riding through the fields and woods and over the hills around Pine Hollow. She knew the land around there pretty well as it was.

"Can everybody hear me?" Max asked. There were fifteen entrants in the junior cross-country. They stood around Max in a circle. "I'm going to go over the rules a final time and then we'll have the draw for positions."

Lisa knew that position could be very important in a ride like this. Whether you went first or last or in the middle could make a difference in your performance. What she couldn't figure out was what position was the best for her. She didn't have time to think about that now. Max had lots to say.

"The course is three miles long. The trail is marked by red stakes. You should have no trouble following it. There are ten obstacles in it. They include two times across the creek, one low jump over a stone wall, one steep climb up a section of hill, and another steep climb down. In addition to these five natural barriers, there are five artificial jumps. Four of them are in the field. One is in the woods. Red and I have ridden the course several times. It's safe and, we think, fun. It's not long. It should take you about fifteen minutes at a steady canter. In fact, it should take you not more than seventeen minutes, nor less than thirteen. Those are your time limits. If you come in either faster or slower, you'll get penalty points. You also get penalty points if your horse refuses an obstacle or if you fall. If you complete the course without a mistake, within the time limit, you don't get any penalty points. Is everything clear?"

The riders nodded and then they all looked around at one another. Lisa had the feeling each of them was wondering if any of them could make it through without a fault. Eventually, it seemed that everybody was looking at Carole.

Max then pulled out a bowl filled with slips of paper containing each rider's name. He began the draw, explaining that two or three riders would be on the course at once and that they'd start at four-minute intervals.

Max reached into the bowl, picked the first scrap of paper, and announced, "Lisa Atwood."

Lisa could feel herself get nervous. It started in her stomach and then traveled quickly to her knees.

"Oh, you poor thing. I hate going first!" the girl next to her said.

On her other side, Stevie gave her a squeeze. "You're so lucky! Just think, you'll be the first person on the trail and you get to set the standard the rest of us have to come up to."

Lisa, who was pretty much of an optimist under any circumstances, decided she liked Stevie's way of looking at the situation. She smiled confidently. The minute she did that, her knees felt better and her stomach steadied.

Then, fifteen minutes later, she was in the starting area.

"Remember," Carole told her reassuringly. "This is a case where it's really true that 'slow and steady wins the race.'"

"Good luck!" Stevie said.

"On your mark," said Mrs. Reg, Max's mother. She was the starter for this event. She checked her timer. "Get set." She pulled a handkerchief out of her pocket and held it high. "Go!" She brought the handkerchief down quickly. Lisa was off.

The course began in the fields behind the stable. Lisa knew the fields well. She looked at the path as it was laid out. It was very level. This, she decided, would be a good time to set the pace she wanted to keep throughout the course. Pepper was cantering, as he was supposed to be, but, she felt, his canter was a little sluggish. When he broke into a trot, she knew that was the case. She signaled him to canter again, by touching behind his girth with her right heel and this time, she also maintained pressure on his belly with her left calf.

It worked. Pepper's canter was an even and smooth rocking gait when he did it right, and it was Lisa's job to make him do it right. She'd accomplished that. She was pleased.

Lisa spotted the first jump. It was only about eighteen inches high. It was eighteen inches across, too. Lisa prepared herself. She shifted her weight a little forward and then, as they approached the jump, she shortened her reins and rose in the saddle, leaning forward, parallel to Pepper's neck. At just the right moment, he rose in the air and cleared the fence handily. Lisa straightened up as Pepper neared the ground and felt herself slide right back into the saddle where she belonged.

"Ten!" she told herself proudly, although in this event, there were no points for doing a good or better or even perfect jump. The idea was to get over it and stay on the horse. She'd accomplished that, too.

The next jump was higher, but not as wide. It was a lot lower than many jumps she'd taken, but it was higher than the last one. Because of that, it seemed to loom a lot higher than she knew it was. The rule of thumb in jumping was that the horse should take off about as far from the jump as it was high. This was almost a three-foot jump. Pepper's front feet should leave the ground about three feet from it. Lisa couldn't help herself. Because the jump looked so high, she got prepared for it too soon. Pepper, always an obedient horse, did exactly what she asked him to do. He took off almost five feet in front of it. Fortunately, he also did what he knew he was supposed to do. He made it over the fence, but just barely. Lisa listened for the sound of a hoof hitting a wooden bar and sighed with relief when she didn't hear it.

"Three!" she said out loud, scoring herself harshly. In a way, though, she felt that the mistake helped her. It reminded her that she could make mistakes—even bad ones—and she'd have to pay attention. She'd been lucky once; she might not be lucky a second time.

After the second jump, the trail turned uphill toward the woods. And there, right before the path entered the woods, was the third obstacle. It was a steep bank about three feet high. The horses couldn't jump it or even go around it. They had to climb it.

Pepper slowed to a walk and, without hesitation, began the climb. Lisa let him do the work. The only thing she had to do was stay in the saddle. To accomplish that, she leaned forward, almost to his neck. Up he went. "Ten," she said, but she knew it was Pepper who had earned it, not her.

The path through the woods and across the creek was a familiar one. She and Stevie and Carole had ridden it many times. On summer days, they liked to stop at the creek, take off their boots, and cool their feet. This was a hot summer day, but there was no time to stop. Pepper looked longingly at the fresh water.

"Later," she told him. "Do what I tell you now, and I'll give you a whole bucketful of water when we get back to the stable." He didn't hesitate. He proceeded right through the shallow, but swift, water and they continued along the trail.

There was a long straightaway ahead, and a jump coming up, Lisa knew. Max hadn't marked the map with the jumps, but logic told her this would be where they would find the first jump set up in the woods. In preparation for it, Lisa brought Pepper to a trot so she could control his canter from the start. She signaled for a canter with one foot and kept the opposite calf on him. It worked like a dream and it paid off when they rounded the bend in the trail. There, just where she'd suspected she would find it, was a two-and-a-half-foot-high jump. Lisa and Pepper sailed right over it.

"Ten," she told Pepper. This time, she took some of the credit for herself.

The trail followed the contour of the hill and then descended again to the creek. Lisa let Pepper walk across it and then began cantering again. She was having such a good time with his pleasant rocking gait that she barely noticed they'd almost reached the field again. Suddenly, Pepper slowed. He'd seen something she hadn't. He'd spotted the sharp descent and if he'd gone at it at a canter, he could have taken a serious tumble. Instead, Lisa was unprepared for the sudden change of gait and she was afraid *she* was going to take a serious tumble.

It wasn't easy to maintain balance when you weren't prepared for a gait change, especially when that also meant the horse was climbing down a sharp hill. Lisa slid forward precariously and tilted off to the right. She clasped with her knees, but she was afraid it was too late. She tried to shorten the reins. She couldn't, though, because Pepper was using his head for balance and he needed freedom of movement. Lisa could feel herself going. She had to do something. She did the only thing she could do. She grabbed onto Pepper's mane and held on for dear life. At that point, she completely lost her seat and she could feel her left leg coming right over the saddle. She was going down!

Then, as suddenly as it had started, it stopped. Pepper had managed to get down the hill and he was standing level, apparently waiting for Lisa to do the same. Quickly, she adjusted the weight on her right stirrup and used that, plus leverage from Pepper's mane, to push herself back up and into the saddle. She found her left stirrup with her toe, settled into her seat, nudged Pepper with her heels, and it was as if nothing had ever happened.

"Nice recovery!" said a voice behind her. Lisa looked over her shoulder. It was Red O'Malley.

"Oh, thanks," she said.

"You're ten minutes out and you've got three to seven minutes to finish the course," he said. "You're doing fine and you'll make it. See you later."

With that, he seemed to disappear behind a bush. That was when Lisa remembered that all of the obstacles had judges at them, checking to make sure that the horses *and* riders made it over or across safely. It was Max's policy to have the judges out of the way. They weren't exactly hiding, but they weren't in obvious places. Lisa had just been so busy giving herself and Pepper scores that she'd forgotten about the judges altogether until Red had spoken. Lisa felt a flush of embarrassment. Then she shrugged her shoulders. What did it matter? She and Pepper had made it over all of the obstacles safely. That's what counted.

Lisa nudged Pepper into a canter. It was slow and easy, just right to clear the next two jumps. Five minutes after she'd seen Red, she rode smoothly across the finish line.

"Go!" Mrs. Reg said to Anna McWhirter, who was just starting the course. Anna and her pony bolted across the starting line, heading for the trail Lisa had just completed.

"How was it?" Stevie asked excitedly. "Did you have any trouble?"

Lisa grinned. "Nah," she said. "It was just like you told me. I set the mark you all have to come up to."

"How many faults?" Stevie asked suspiciously.

"None," Lisa told her.

"I knew you could do it!" Carole said. She leaned over from her perch on Starlight and gave Lisa a hug. "This is your event!"

"Oh, you'll both do wonderfully, too," Lisa said. "And I wish I could be out on the course watching you."

"No, there's something more important you have to do," Stevie said.

"Oh, what's that?" Lisa asked. She was suspicious because the look on Stevie's face said it was something mysterious. Then Lisa remembered that there *was* something mysterious going on—the horsenapping.

"Stevie, you're next!" Max said sharply.

"Wish me luck!" Stevie said, waving to Lisa and Carole.

"You've got it!" Carole assured her.

Carole watched Lisa walk her horse to cool him down near the starting line waiting for Stevie to get the go-ahead signal. While they waited, Lisa told them both as much as she could about the trail and the obstacles. She particularly warned them about the downhill obstacle coming out of the woods. Then, Lisa and Carole cheered Stevie on until Mrs. Reg's handkerchief flew downward and Stevie headed for the first jump. The last thing Lisa and Carole saw before Stevie was out of sight was that she was aimed too far to the right for the first jump.

"Oh, no," Lisa said.

"Don't worry," Carole told her. "Stevie will do just fine. She always thinks of everything. Now, here's what she's thought of for you . . ."

CAROLE WAS HAVING a hard time. It was easy for her to tell herself that this was Starlight's first competition and he'd do better in the future. That was something that was easy to say, but it wasn't very comforting. Starlight wasn't doing well and Carole was sure it was her fault.

He'd refused one jump because he'd been startled by a butterfly just before he was supposed to jump. Then, he'd insisted on getting something to drink in the creek. Both times, Carole thought she saw the judge pursing her lips. That was all she needed! Taking a drink in the creek amounted to a refusal. Now, about halfway through the course, Starlight was suddenly hurrying. She'd have to bring him in at a walk not to beat the time, and walking on the open trail was breaking gait under Max's rules. That meant another fault.

"It's okay, boy. I know you're doing your best. You did okay yesterday. You just like the showy events better, with lots of people in the ring to admire you, right?"

As if to answer her, Starlight approached the next jump smoothly and cleared it by at least two feet.

"Ahh," Carole said. "You've heard that there will be jumping tomorrow. You want to win that one? Okay, then, I'll give you a chance. But for now, let's finish up properly. I want a nice, even canter."

Starlight responded to her voice. Max always told his riders that their horses couldn't understand English. And although Carole thought there were some things they understood very well indeed, they all understood tone of voice. Carole suspected that Starlight was as disappointed in his performance as she was in hers. He seemed glad to know she wasn't angry with him. Now she looked at her watch and held her breath. According to her watch, she'd been on the trail for twelve and a half minutes. Would it be possible for Starlight to take thirty seconds to cross the short stretch of field to the finish line at a canter? She held her breath.

"Thirteen minutes, fifteen seconds," Max said as she crossed the finish line.

Carole let out her breath. She might have more than a few jump faults, but at least she and Starlight had made it in within the time limit.

Carole dismounted and walked Starlight around the

paddock to cool him down. Several of the other riders were doing the same thing. She expected to see Stevie there, too, but she wasn't in sight.

As she came around the second time, she saw both of her friends, standing at the fence. At first, she thought they were waving to her, but they weren't. They were waving *at* her. They obviously wanted to talk to her. Maybe they'd heard about her poor performance on the cross-country course and they wanted to console her. She was fine, though, really. She just waved back.

The flailing arms didn't stop. Carole turned Starlight around and walked to her friends.

"It's Veronica!" Stevie hissed.

"Yeah, she's not there!" Lisa added.

This didn't make much sense to Carole. Right before she'd left on the cross-country course, she'd told Lisa that she should call Veronica, on some pretext. The girls wanted her to talk to Veronica to see if, by any chance, the horsenappers had gotten in touch with her. If they had called Veronica, then it was a sure bet they'd called everybody and then there would be nothing The Saddle Club could do to help the horses. It would be totally in the hands of the owners and, maybe, the police.

"What are you talking about?" Carole asked.

"I called Veronica, just like you said," Lisa began. "But she wasn't there."

"So?"

Carole still couldn't see anything to be worried about. But when Lisa continued, Carole understood. "I spoke with their housekeeper. It turns out that Mr. and Mrs. diAngelo are out of town for the day. So, the housekeeper is in charge of Veronica. She sounded totally frantic when I asked for Veronica and started blurting out all kinds of things, but the gist of it was that Veronica is missing! The housekeeper said she'd disappeared right after breakfast and they hadn't heard a word from her and they are terribly worried."

"Yeah," Stevie said. "What if these creeps aren't just horsenappers? Like, they think they've struck it rich when they realize they actually have *the* horse belonging to *the* diAngelos, so they get greedy and decide to swipe their daughter, too."

"Veronica? Kidnapped?" Carole said numbly as the idea sank in.

"Wait a minute," Lisa said. "The maid didn't say anything about a ransom note. We don't *know* she's been kidnapped . . ."

"But we don't know she hasn't been!" Stevie said.

"Can we take the chance?" Carole asked. "I mean, if both her parents are out of town, who *is* there to help her?"

"I think we'd better have a Saddle Club meeting and we'd better not have it right here," Stevie said, glancing around. "The paddocks have ears!"

Carole decided Starlight had cooled down enough.

She put him in his stall, cross-tied him, loosened his girth, and the three girls headed for the hayloft. It was a quiet place where they could talk without anybody over-hearing them. Stevie moved bales of hay around so they could sit in a close circle.

"Come on," she invited her friends. "We have to figure out what to do."

"It's obvious what we have to do," Lisa said. "We have to figure out if Veronica really was kidnapped."

"We don't have time for that," Stevie said. "We have to assume she was and save her. Otherwise, it might be too late."

"Fine, fine," Carole agreed. "But just how do you propose to save her? We don't even know where to begin looking."

"Well, I've been thinking about that," Stevie said. "See, the way I figure it, the horses, and Veronica, have to be nearby. I wasn't absolutely sure of that until Veronica disappeared. The horsenappers would only have taken Veronica if they'd been in the area. Otherwise, they wouldn't have risked coming back. So, they're here, and what does that mean?"

"Willow Creek's a pretty small town," Lisa reminded Stevie.

"Yes, so there's no way they can be hanging out in any of the houses or farms. We know everybody. Somebody would notice them. Therefore, they're not in a house."

"Therefore, they're hiding out in the woods," Carole said.

"Precisely!" Stevie announced. "So let's go find them!"

"How?" Lisa asked.

"Horseback, of course," Carole said.

"Of course," Stevie said, her eyes gleaming with excitement.

"Of course," Lisa concluded.

THE GIRLS QUICKLY saddled their horses and prepared to ride into the woods. The trouble was, there were a lot of woods in Willow Creek. In fact, there was a whole state forest there, crisscrossed with trails that led to all kinds of remote places.

"Where on earth are we going to go?" Lisa asked logically.

"I don't know if this is right, but I do know it makes sense," Carole began. "If I were going to hide horses and needed access by road, plus essentials like fresh water, I'd take them to the rock quarry."

"Hey," Stevie said, genuinely impressed. "That makes good sense. It makes especially good sense because the woods right near Pine Hollow are filled with cross-country riders now. Smart horsenappers wouldn't want to have their hideout turn out to be on the trail of forty or fifty riders! So, let's check it out."

The rock quarry was on the other side of the road from Pine Hollow. Whenever the girls rode on trails in the woods, they generally stayed on the Pine Hollow side, the one Max had chosen for the cross-country course, but Stevie had lived all of her life in Willow Creek and knew the entire forest very well. "Follow me," she said. They did.

They took the road for about a hundred yards and then turned left on a fire road that led into the forest. The fire road was wide enough for all three girls to ride abreast.

"You know, it's a funny thing, but I feel kind of sorry for Veronica," Stevie remarked.

"I often do," Lisa said. "Anyone who behaves that horribly must be a very unhappy person."

Carole looked at her. "I never really thought of it that way," she said. "I've only ever felt sorry for her horses, but I suppose we *should* feel sorry for her."

"That isn't what I meant," Stevie interjected. "I don't feel sorry because she behaves horribly. She's had all kinds of chances to learn to behave better and she's got everything in the world a girl could need to be happy, so there's no excuse for her to misbehave and be unhappy. I actually was referring to the fact that being kidnapped probably isn't exactly swell fun."

"You don't suppose the kidnappers have tied her up, do you?" Lisa asked.

"I don't know about tied up, but if they've got any sense, they've got her gagged," Stevie said, showing less sympathy than she had just a few minutes before.

"If I were Veronica, the worst part would be knowing that they could hurt my horse," Carole said. The thought made her lean forward and pat Starlight reassuringly on his neck.

"Remember, though," Stevie said, "this is the girl who wanted to turn her horse into dog food."

"I don't think she really meant it. How could anyone?" Carole asked Stevie.

"In Veronica's case—hey, look at that!" Stevie said, pointing to the ground. She drew Topside to a halt. Lisa and Carole stopped to look, too, but they didn't see anything. Stevie dismounted and walked forward slowly, holding Topside's reins. If she was trying to look like an Iroquois tracker, Carole thought she was doing a pretty good job of it. Curious, Carole and Lisa dismounted as well.

"What is it?" Carole asked.

Then Stevie did something that only Stevie could get away with. She fished around in her pocket and pulled out a magnifying glass. "I told you we'd need this, didn't I?"

Lisa stifled a giggle. "Okay, Sherlock, what's up?" she asked.

Stevie held the glass close to the ground. "Aha, just as I thought!" she said.

"One more 'aha' and I'm going to be sick," Lisa said. "Why don't you just tell us what you're looking at?"

Stevie stood up. "Well," she said. "It rained night before last, before the event started. And then, remember how the ground was soft and muddy the first day of the event?" Lisa and Carole nodded. "Sometime after the rain, but before the ground got hard again, something heavy went over this roadway."

"Hey, it's a tire track!" Carole said, just spotting what Stevie had seen from the start.

Then Lisa saw it, too. "Oh!" she said. "But how do we know it's our horsenappers?"

"We don't," Stevie said. "We just know that something went over this trail yesterday. It's a possibility that that something was a horse trailer."

"So it's a possibility that we're on the right trail," Carole concluded.

"We'd better be careful," Lisa said. Her friends agreed. They remounted their horses and proceeded.

It was easy then for the girls to follow the trail of the tire tracks. When the road forked, the tracks clearly went to the left. That didn't surprise the girls. That was the way to the quarry. But when they got to the creek, there was a surprise.

"They stop!" Stevie said. "No more tire tracks on the other side of the creek."

This time, Carole dismounted and looked carefully at the ground. She felt a little silly. After all, she was no pioneer tracker. She spurned Stevie's offer of the magnifying glass.

"I don't see any sign of anything here," she said at last. "Except some careless campers." She picked up a gum wrapper and put it in her pocket. "I hate it when people do that."

"I hate it more when a trail simply stops," Stevie said.

Lisa scratched her head. "Look," she said. "Maybe we were making a wrong assumption that the tracks we've been following were made by a horse trailer. Maybe the tracks didn't have anything to do with the horsenapping at all. That doesn't mean Carole wasn't right in the first place that the horses are in the quarry. I think we still ought to look there, don't you?"

"Yes, of course," Stevie said enthusiastically. "And maybe the tracks stopping were actually intended to confuse us!"

Carole didn't think that was likely and she told Stevie so.

"You have no idea of all the clever things criminals do to confound great detectives," Stevie said.

Carole thought Stevie was probably right about that,

but she had the funniest feeling Stevie didn't have much of an idea about great detectives, either. She kept the thought to herself.

The girls got back on their horses and Stevie led the way along the now narrow trail to the rock quarry.

About a hundred yards from the quarry, The Saddle Club dismounted, hitched their horses to a tree, and proceeded to the quarry by crouching and creeping as silently as they could manage. They didn't want to alert the horsenappers to their approach.

"How far?" Lisa whispered.

"Shhhh!" Carole hissed.

"Oomph!" Stevie grunted, tripping over a root.

"Shhhhhhhh!" Carole and Lisa said together.

"It hurts!" Stevie declared loudly, rubbing her knee.

"It'll hurt more if we get discovered," Lisa warned her.

"There's nobody there," Stevie said.

"How do you know?" Carole asked.

"Because we've been making enough noise to alert even the densest horsenapper to our presence."

Carole and Lisa stood up and walked into the quarry. Stevie was absolutely right. There was no sign of life there, especially no sign of horsenappers.

"Not even a bale of hay," Carole said in dismay.

"It was still a good guess," Lisa said, trying to console Carole.

"No, it wasn't," Stevie said matter-of-factly. "It was a nice try, but it wasn't a good guess because it was wrong."

"You're just cranky because your knee hurts," Lisa said.

"No, I'm just cranky because this didn't work," Stevie said. Then she relented a little. "I'm sorry, Carole. It *was* a good guess."

"Not good enough," Carole said, and they all knew that was true.

Disappointed, they remounted their horses and headed back the way they'd come.

"I've got an idea," Lisa said. "When we finish grooming our horses, I think we should go over to TD's"—the local ice cream parlor—"and have a Saddle Club meeting. That's where we usually have them and it's where we do some of our best horse-talking. Maybe a hot-fudge sundae will inspire our brain cells to figure out exactly what the horsenappers have done with the horses."

"Maybe it will inspire our brain cells to figure out exactly how we're going to tell a whole bunch of grown-ups exactly how long we've known about the horsenapping and haven't told anybody," Stevie said.

"How do you think hot fudge will do on the answer to the 'Exactly-how-long-have-you-known-Veronica-was-kidnapped?' question?" Carole asked.

"Yeah, that one could be problematical," Lisa agreed.

"Especially if something happens to her," Stevie said.

"That's an awful thought," Carole agreed. "Even for Veronica. I mean, we've all been tempted to do something awful to her from time to time, but then we always knew—"

"Shhhh!" Stevie said, suddenly drawing Topside to a halt. Pepper and Starlight stopped on Stevie's signal, too.

"What is it?" Lisa asked.

Stevie shook her head. She didn't know. "I heard something," she said. "It sounded like a horse."

The girls stood silently. Carole watched Starlight's ears, knowing that his good hearing would be even more alert to the sounds of another horse than hers would be.

"Who's there?" a voice called out from around the bend of the trail, where it crossed the creek.

"Who's *there*?" Stevie countered cleverly.

"It's me!" the voice called back.

"Well, it's us," Stevie answered. Carole could see the proud grin on her face. She loved games like this. Carole hoped this was a game.

"It's Donald!" the voice called. "Is that you girls? Stevie? Uh, Carole? And, um—"

"Lisa!" she called out. She didn't like to be forgotten.

"Yeah, right. Lisa." His horse rounded the bend. "There you are!" he said.

"What are you doing here?" Stevie challenged him.

"Looking for you. Is everything all right?"

"Of course it's all right!" Stevie said. "Did you think

we'd be in trouble riding in these woods? Why, I've lived here all my life. I know these woods like the back of my hand. There's no way I could get lost. Besides, we're not even that far from Pine Hollow and . . ."

"Okay, okay," Donald said. "I'm just glad to know everything's okay with you. I saw you all take off and when you didn't come back right away, I was worried about you. So, when Max told me to take a break, I wanted to make sure you were okay. Do you mind?"

Stevie was surprised. Lisa was confused. Carole was touched.

"That's awfully nice of you, Donald," she said. "You've been working so hard these past couple of days because of the event. You didn't have to follow us in here. We're okay. See, we were looking for a trail—a track, really."

Stevie couldn't believe her ears. If she was hearing things right, Carole was about to tell Donald what they were up to. That was a bad idea. This was a Saddle Club project, not a stablehand project. She cut Carole off before she spilled the beans.

"Yes, a track," she said. "Carole had this idea that there was a little railroad track in the old quarry, so they could run little cars out of there with granite on them. We rode all the way there and didn't see a thing. So, if there is a track there, it's a total secret to the whole wide world."

Stevie made sure to stress the last few words. Carole got the hint.

"Yes," she agreed. "It's still a secret."

"Very secret," Lisa added.

Donald looked at them all quizzically. "I promise to keep your secret a secret," he said. "But now, I think you'd better get back to Pine Hollow."

"That's where we were headed," Stevie told him. "Are you going back now too?"

Donald nodded. He turned his horse around and retreated along the trail. The girls followed him in single file. They didn't talk as they rode. There was an awful lot to talk about, but it would all have to wait until they got to TD's.

"Oh, no, it's you!" the waitress at TD's said, wincing at the sight of Stevie.

Stevie shrugged innocently, as if she couldn't imagine what upset the waitress so much. Lisa and Carole giggled. They knew exactly what upset the woman. Stevie had a well-earned reputation for ordering awful mixtures of sundaes. Stevie always seemed to love what she ordered, no matter how unlikely the combination was, but those around her always suspected she just ordered them so nobody else would want tastes.

The waitress put down glasses of water and told the girls she'd be back in a minute to take their orders. Carole had the funniest feeling the woman was just trying to put off the inevitable.

The three of them were sitting in their favorite booth

in the back of TD's. Carole and Lisa sat next to each other. Stevie was across from them, facing the door of the restaurant.

"Wasn't that sweet of Donald to come after us in the woods?" Lisa said.

Stevie shook her head. "No, it was annoying." The words sounded a little harsh to her. "Well, I suppose it was a little sweet, but I can't figure out why he did it. Everybody knows we wouldn't get lost. Besides that, I doubt Max gave him more than a ten-minute break. It must have taken him forty-five minutes to find us and come back with us. I'm sure Max wasn't too pleased by that."

Lisa leaned forward and put her elbows on the table. "Maybe not, but he must have been awfully pleased with all the work Donald's been getting done these last few days. I've never seen anybody run as fast carrying tack as he does."

"Awfully fast," Carole agreed. "But remember how careless he was with the wheelbarrow around Topside? Sometimes he seems terrific. Other times he just seems terrifically rushed. I can't make him out. Can you, Stevie?"

"Hmmm?" Stevie looked up distractedly from the menu she'd picked up. "Did you know they have a new flavor? White chocolate almond?"

Carole was a little annoyed that Stevie was more inter-

74

ested in the menu than she was in Carole's thoughts about Donald, but she dismissed her irritation. They had all worked hard and deserved a treat. And creating treats at TD's was a lot of work for Stevie.

"So, how are we going to tell people about the horses?" Lisa asked, coming to the subject.

"And about Veronica?" Carole added. "Stevie?" she asked, trying to draw Stevie's attention from the menu, which, aside from white chocolate almond, never changed much.

"Right," Stevie said, putting down the menu. "What are we going to tell them? Well, with any luck, we won't have to tell them."

"How's that?" Lisa asked.

"One of two things will happen," Stevie said. "The first is that the horsenappers will get in touch with the diAngelos again and/or with Alicia or Mr. Feeney, and somebody will pay the ransom and then that person and/or those people may and/or may not get his or her horse back but that doesn't matter because once the diAngelos know, then the cat is out of the bag because Alicia and Mr. Feeney already know and the only thing that will ever be a mystery is what happened to the first note from the horsenappers?"

Carole looked at Lisa. "Did you follow that?" she asked.

Lisa nodded. "But wait, there's more."

"And the other thing that could happen is that we will discover the whereabouts of the three horses and Veronica and we'll manage it in a way that nobody will ever know that we knew that something was wrong."

"I like that one better," Carole said. "We get to be heroines." Thoughts of photographs in newspapers, awards, and rewards floated through her mind. She was about to share those thoughts with her friends when they were interrupted.

"Ready to order?" the waitress asked. The girls nodded.

Lisa ordered first. "I'll have a dish of chocolate mint chip," she said. The waitress nodded and jotted down the order.

"I'll have a small hot fudge on vanilla," Carole said. The waitress wrote that down, too.

All eyes turned to Stevie, whose eyes seemed to be glued to something behind Carole and Lisa.

"Vanilla," Stevie said.

Everybody was surprised, but the most surprised appeared to be Stevie. The waitress disappeared before Stevie could say anything else.

"What's the matter?" Lisa asked. She'd never known Stevie to order plain vanilla before.

"Yeah, what is it?" Carole asked.

"Veronica," Stevie said numbly.

"Just because Veronica is missing you're changing the way you eat?" Carole asked.

"No, not because she's missing," Stevie said, still apparently staring off into space. "Because she isn't." Then Carole and Lisa turned around and looked where Stevie had been looking. There, sauntering into TD's, was none other than Veronica diAngelo.

"No ropes, no gag," Stevie said.

"There isn't even a tough guy behind her holding a gun," Lisa observed.

"No apparent bruising," Carole added.

"She's wearing her hair a little differently," Lisa said. "She doesn't usually pull it up and away from her face like that."

"There must be a reason," Carole said.

"But it probably doesn't have to do with kidnappers," Stevie concluded.

Veronica continued her sauntering, right over to The Saddle Club's table. "Well, hello," she greeted them all too sweetly. "Are you all done showing off for today?" She glared at Stevie, still unable to forgive her for the turn on the forehand she'd performed for the judges yesterday.

"Well, yes," Stevie replied just as sweetly, and just as insincerely. "And are you all done with your furious tantrums—or have you given up on them now that Mumsy and Daddykins are out of town and can't hear them?"

A puzzled look crossed Veronica's face. "How did you know that?" she asked.

Carole thought that was a tricky question. They couldn't reveal that they'd called Veronica because there would have been no reasonable excuse for them to have done so. Veronica would smell a rat for sure. Carole was concerned that Stevie was skating pretty close to the edge of trouble. But Stevie had the answer.

"We know everything," she said simply. "We even know that your housekeeper was worried about you when you left the house this morning and didn't say where you were going."

That was the distraction Veronica needed. "Oh, that busybody!" she declared. Even from Veronica that seemed extreme, Carole thought. After all, the housekeeper was supposed to be in charge of Veronica while her parents were away. "She must have called Pine Hollow to see if I was there—as if I would be after my horse messed up so badly yesterday. Well, it serves her right if she was worried. All I did was leave the house early to do a little shopping."

Then, she turned on her heel and strode away. While The Saddle Club watched, Veronica glanced around TD's looking to see if any of her clique were there. They were not. She then spurned the hostess's offer of a menu and stormed out of the place.

"Shopping?" Stevie said. "That girl has an infinite capacity to amaze me."

"Now I understand the new hairdo," Lisa said.

"You do?" Carole asked.

"Sure, see, her mother has a charge account at the jewelry store here at the shopping center. I don't know where else she was today, but while Mumsy and Daddykins are away, the little mouse was playing—among the jewels. Did you notice her new earrings?"

"I must confess that I never notice anything about Veronica except how much I dislike her," Stevie said. "And every time I have to talk to her, I just get all wound up in trying to be snootier than she is. Anyway, no, I didn't notice her earrings."

"I did," Carole said. "They were garnets, weren't they?"

"Yes," Lisa said.

"And I suspect she didn't buy garnets because they reminded her of her beautiful horse. I suspect she bought them because she thought the color of the stones would match the color of the horse."

"Now, that's what I call accessorizing!" Stevie joked.

"I bet it's what Veronica calls accessorizing, too," Carole said. "Only, in her case, she's not joking about it."

"Chocolate mint chip?" the waitress asked.

"That's me," Lisa told her.

"Hot fudge—" she put the dish in front of Carole— "and the plain vanilla," she said, slipping that dish in front of Stevie.

Stevie looked at it, puzzled. "You forgot something, didn't you?" she asked.

"That's what you ordered," the woman said patiently.

"I know I did," Stevie said. "But I also wanted a scoop of pistachio and some of the blueberry topping and if you could put some pineapple topping on the vanilla . . ."

Stevie stopped talking because the woman was running away. She shook her head. "Funny place, this. They never want to give you what you really want." Then she picked up her spoon and began eating plain vanilla.

CAROLE, LISA, AND Stevie stood at the entrance to the ring and stared in disbelief.

"We're actually going to have to jump all of those, in order?" Lisa said.

Carole nodded. While they watched, Max, Mrs. Reg, Donald, and Red O'Malley set up the jumps for the junior stadium event. There were eight jumps, but that included eleven obstacles because one of the jumps was a double jump and another was a triple.

"I'll never make it," Lisa said.

"Yes, you will," Stevie told her. "Think of it as something you'll do for the glory of The Saddle Club."

Lisa gave her a wry look. "No, I'll think of it as something I do to keep myself from being humiliated."

"This from somebody—the *only* somebody—who had a perfect score on the cross-country course?" Stevie teased.

"Well, you know, it's not so much that the jumps are high, or even that they're difficult, but the course is so complicated."

Stevie smiled. "And she's the A-student in the group, isn't she?" she asked Carole.

Carole barely heard her. Carole was watching the process in the arena with every ounce of her attention. "Look, all the jumps are numbered and as soon as they're set up, we can go walk the course. That should help us remember the order."

"All we have to do is get over them in order, right?" Lisa asked.

"Not quite," Carole said. "See, usually with this kind of event, that's all there is to it, as long as you do it within a time limit. But here at Pine Hollow, the rules are made by Max and he expects more of his junior riders. He wants us to do it in good form, too. We have to keep our horses at an even pace and we have to jump properly. We'll get penalty points if we make stylistic errors, like letting our arms flap or trotting on the wrong diagonal."

"Max sure expects a lot from us, doesn't he?" Stevie said.

"Yes," Carole agreed. "That's why he's such a good teacher."

This was the morning of the final day of Pine Hollow's three-day event, and the jumping was the last competition for the junior riders. The adult competition would be after lunch and then the ribbons would be awarded and all the competitors would ride in the closing-ceremony parade. It was a big day for The Saddle Club in more than one sense. It was also the last day they'd given themselves to find the missing horses. That was important; they all knew that. But first things came first and what came first today was the jumping competition.

"All right, now. It's time to walk the course," Max announced.

Those were the words Carole had been waiting to hear. She took one of the maps that Mrs. Reg was handing out to the riders and studied it first. The course was complicated, zigzagging back and forth along the full length of the field, but as Carole studied it, she began to see the logic of the layout. The whole course was designed to test all of the skills Max had had his students working on since the first day they'd each been in a saddle. This wasn't so much a competition against other riders as it was a test of each individual rider's skills. She folded the map, put it in her pocket, and began to study the real thing.

According to the schedule, Max allowed the riders to spend fifteen minutes studying the course. Carole used all of it. She walked the route several times, measuring the distances between the jumps with strides so she'd have an idea of how many strides Starlight would need to take. That way, she could also plan how far in front of each jump he would take off. She made a mental note of all the landmarks to help her remember everything.

Before Carole could believe it, the whistle blew. It was time to mount up and warm Starlight up, too. She'd drawn number six for this event, so at least she would have the advantage of watching five other riders, including Stevie, go through the course before it was her turn. She intended to make good use of that advantage.

"Hello, Carole, are you there?" It was Stevie. She was standing next to Carole, waving her hand in front of Carole's face to get her attention. Carole blinked.

"Oh," she said. "I'm sorry. I've just been concentrating."

"That's obvious," Stevie told her. "Did you learn anything?"

"I learned a zillion things, made notes to myself about exactly where I want to begin all the jumps, where I need to change leads, how fast I think Starlight should be going with each approach, and how many strides he'll need to take between each of the jumps."

84

"Wow," Stevie said, genuinely impressed.

"But the trouble is that I don't think I'll remember any of it."

"You'll do fine," Stevie said. "I've watched Starlight jump enough to know that this is his event."

"I hope so," Carole said.

"Well, let's go tighten our horses' girths and get this over with." Together, they entered the stable.

Lisa was there, giving Pepper a final brushing, and dusting some sawdust off his rump.

"I don't know about this one, guys," Lisa said.

"No problem," Stevie said. "At least not for us. This is going to be Carole's event. The best we can do is the best we can do. Carole and Starlight are going to take it, cold. See, now the pressure's off. Feel better?"

Lisa laughed. "You know I do," she said. "You always have that effect on me."

The girls finished the final grooming and tacking process and met in the hallway. Then they examined one anothers' horses to be sure their tack was spotless and their horses' coats were shiny. They had all done their work. It was time to warm up the horses and get ready for the competition.

Stevie was second. Lisa and Carole stood by the edge of the ring and crossed their fingers for her. Topside had once belonged to a championship rider and he had been in competition all of his adult life. He knew what he was doing. So did Stevie. Unfortunately, so did Max. The jump course was a tricky one that tested the rider and the horse. Stevie was good, but a few of the jump combinations were better than she was.

"It's the triple that will get the riders," Carole said. "See, it's not that they are high jumps. They aren't. It's that they are close together and your horse has to be completely balanced and cantering rhythmically before he can take off again. Max hasn't left us much space between those jumps for recovery."

Stevie sailed smoothly over the first three jumps. She grinned as she passed her friends. Carole had the feeling Stevie wanted to wave, but of course she couldn't do that. That was definitely not good form. Then she approached the triple combination. Topside was in top form. Stevie had him take off at just the right moment and he recovered almost instantly for the second part of it. Again, no problem. The third jump was as good as the first two. Carole and Lisa automatically began applauding and they weren't alone. Everyone in the audience did, too.

"She seems so relaxed," Lisa said.

"Too relaxed," Carole said. "If she's not careful, she's going to—"

And then Stevie got into trouble. She let Topside take a slow curve approach to the next jump and instead of aiming straight at it, they came at an angle. Stevie misjudged her distance and Topside took off too close to the jump. Topside's hoof caught the top bar on the way over, knocking it to the ground.

"That's five faults," Carole said.

"But so far, those are her only faults," Lisa reminded her.

Carole knew that was true, but she also could tell that Stevie had gotten rattled. She was distracted and it cost her. She got too close to the next jump before signaling Topside for the takeoff and he refused the jump. Stevie knew what to do. She circled around and brought him back through the approach. This time, they went right over it, but the refusal cost another ten faults.

Stevie had learned her lesson about concentration. From there until the end of the competition, she and Topside worked together as if they'd been born together. It was a great finish. It had been a great start, too. It was only the middle that worried Carole.

"You were great!" Lisa said, greeting her back at the fence.

"I wasn't, but thanks anyway," Stevie told her.

Carole gave her a hug. "You were great part of the time," she said truthfully. "You took that triple like a pro and your finale was really grand."

"And the middle wasn't so hot," Stevie said, evaluating herself honestly.

"But you recovered and that's really important. It may

not get you a blue ribbon, but it certainly does get you respect."

Stevie dismounted and gave Topside the pat that he deserved. "I don't want a blue ribbon on this anyway. It's yours to win," she told Carole. "Good luck."

"Thanks," Carole said.

"I'm going to cool down Topside and put him in his stall. I'll be back in time for your turn, okay?" Stevie asked. Carole and Lisa nodded and then turned their attention to the next competitor.

"Look at her hands," Carole said. "They're all over the place. She's never going to—" The first jump was down.

Stevie walked Topside back to his stall. She wasn't thrilled with her performance, but she was proud of the fact that she'd pulled herself back together after a few mistakes. Sometimes that was hard to do. Riding a great horse like Topside made it easier. As she walked, she told him all the wonderful things she'd do for him when she had time. Her promises included carrots and two-hour showers. He followed her willingly.

The stable was quite deserted. Everybody was watching the jumping. So, Stevie was more than a little surprised to hear somebody talking agitatedly. She halted Topside and listened.

There was a phone in the stable. It was only supposed to be used for emergencies, but a lot of people defined emergencies for their own convenience. From the tone of voice Stevie heard from around the corner, this person had definitely defined his problem as an emergency. He was speaking in a nervous whisper that made it impossible to identify the voice. There was no mistaking the urgency of the tone, though.

"Of course I've got to have the money! And I've got to have it now . . ."

Stevie didn't want to barge in on that. Whoever was talking on the phone obviously had a problem and probably didn't want anybody else to know about it.

"Look, I've done what I had to do . . . I've been busting my gut getting everything—"

Topside whinnied. Since all of the other horses were out, waiting to compete, the person on the phone knew somebody was near and apparently didn't like the idea.

"Look, I can't talk now," he said, and then Stevie heard the phone being cradled.

Stevie was embarrassed to have overheard what she had overheard. She was also dying of curiosity. Anybody who was that desperate for cash could do anything. Was it possible that there was a horsenapper lurking around the corner?

Stevie clucked her tongue to get Topside walking again. They rounded the corner, and although Stevie could see clear to the end of the hallway, there wasn't a sign of anybody. The telephone talker had disappeared altogether.

Topside went into his stall willingly. Stevie loosened his girth and brought him a bucket of water and some fresh hay. She cross-tied him.

"See you later, boy," she said. She fastened the door to his stall behind her.

Then, as she headed back toward the ring, Donald went whizzing past her, carrying clean tack. He nodded a quick greeting. It occurred to her that he might have seen something—or someone.

"Oh, Donald," she said. "Did you see somebody here just a few minutes ago?"

He paused and looked at her thoughtfully. "Nope," he said. "The place has been deserted since the junior jumping began." Then he disappeared as quickly as he'd appeared.

Stevie shrugged. It wasn't surprising, really, that Donald hadn't seen the person who'd been talking on the phone. He was always dashing one place or another and didn't ever seem to see anything!

Stevie looked at the phone as she passed it again, almost hoping that it would tell her something. All it told her, though, was that one of the hundreds of people who'd been tromping through the stable had been careless, for there was a gum wrapper dropped on a bale of hay.

"You'd think people would be more careful," she said, picking up the scrap of paper automatically and pocketing it until she found a wastebasket. "Goats eat paper," she said to herself. "But that stuff could make a horse sick!"

10

"GOOD LUCK, CAROLE," Lisa said, and gave her a squeeze. Then she showed her crossed fingers. "We're rooting for you."

"Yes, we are," Stevie said, joining Lisa at the entrance to the ring. She crossed her fingers, too.

Carole thought that, with friends like that, she couldn't lose.

"You're on!" Mrs. Reg said, wishing her luck. The gong sounded. It was time to begin.

Carole entered the ring and, as with the dressage, she saluted the judges. She then had a full minute to begin the course and she intended to use it. This was Starlight's first time jumping in an arena before a crowd. She wanted to accustom him to the atmosphere and the people. They circled the ring at a trot and approached the long straightaway that ended in the first jump. This was exactly the way Carole had planned her route. At the corner, when Starlight was aimed for the jump, she signaled him to canter. He responded instantly. Starlight's canter was pure magic as far as Carole was concerned. It could carry her away anywhere, anytime, but not this time. This time, she had to concentrate completely on the task in front of her and Starlight. She was convinced that she had the most wonderful horse in the event and she wanted everybody else to know it, too.

Carole's work in the ring walking the course paid off right away. She knew just how long the straightaway was and she remembered that she'd decided Starlight should take off for his jump when they reached the slightly crooked pole in the fence. She was ready. So was he. He took off perfectly and sailed right over the jump. When they were above the jump and beginning their descent, Carole straightened up a little and slid back into the saddle, meeting it smoothly as Starlight's hooves met the ground. He cantered on immediately and she never felt the least bit out of balance. The audience applauded. Carole knew she deserved it. She also knew Starlight deserved it.

"Good boy," she whispered to him.

The next two jumps were just as smooth and then came the triple combination. Starlight took stock of the three jumps ahead of him as they cantered toward the obstacles. Carole knew what she wanted Starlight to do and it seemed to her that she almost didn't have to tell him. He responded instantly to her wishes. Almost before she knew what had happened, she and her horse had cleared them perfectly.

"Ooooh!" the audience said, and then clapped.

For a second, Carole listened to the applause. Then she recalled how distracting that had been for Stevie and how much trouble it had caused her. Carole shut it out of her mind and kept her attention glued to the next jump, and then the one after it and the double combination after that. Before she really knew what was happening, Carole and Starlight cleared the last jump flawlessly and rode smoothly through the finish line. She drew her horse down to a trot and returned to the center of the ring, where she gave a final salute to the judges.

When she lifted her head, she saw that people were standing. They were standing and applauding her and Starlight. Carole was embarrassed. She'd been riding for a long time and it had always been important to her to do it well, but she'd always done it well for herself. Other people's opinions, except for her instructors', had never mattered to her. Now, there she was in the middle of the jump course at Pine Hollow and over a hundred people were standing and applauding the way she and Starlight had performed. She didn't have any idea what to do. She looked over at her friends for help. Her friends were clapping as hard as anyone else. Carole touched the brim of her hat to salute the audience and then signaled Starlight to trot out of the ring. He just about pranced. Carole thought he deserved the chance to show off.

Lisa and Stevie greeted her at the gate. "You were fabulous!" Stevie shrieked.

Carole dismounted. Lisa gave her a great big hug. "You stopped the whole show!" she said.

"It wasn't me," Carole tried to tell them. "It was Starlight. He was just born to jump!" She paused, then continued. "And maybe I was born to make him jump."

Stevie and Lisa gave her another round of hugs.

"When are you up?" Carole asked, suddenly realizing that the event hadn't stopped just because she'd finished.

"After this rider," Lisa said.

"Are you nervous?" Carole asked.

"Not at all," Lisa said. "I was, up until your turn. But then you did such a wonderful job, I know there's no way I could possibly do that well, so I don't have to worry about it. I can just go out and do my best and that's all that I have to do."

"That's all you should ever have to do," Carole said.

"I know," Lisa told her. She was going to say something else, but Mrs. Reg called her name. "I guess it's time to go do it."

"Good luck," Carole and Stevie called at the same time. Then they stood together and watched Lisa enter the ring.

"She'll do fine," Carole said.

"I know," Stevie told her. "And we can help her by standing here and crossing our fingers."

Lisa did do a good job. She was still a novice rider and only had limited experience as a jumper, but she'd learned a lot in the short time she'd been doing it and riding an experienced horse like Pepper helped, too. She worked hard to keep Pepper cantering at a steady pace and she was careful with her own form, holding her hands and elbows close to her body, keeping her back straight, and bending from her hips, not her waist.

She did make some mistakes, though, and they added on a few faults. On one jump, she waited to jump until she and Pepper were too close. Pepper brought down the top bar of the jump with him. Then, on the triple, she got into some real trouble. The problem, for Lisa, was that the jumps were too close together and she didn't have time to collect herself, or her horse, before she had to jump again. Both she and Pepper seemed to get confused. He knocked over the second jump of the combination and refused the third altogether. Lisa turned him around and made him approach the combination a second time. Then he made it over, but it had cost her lots of faults.

Carole could see the determination on Lisa's face. She thought she knew what was going through Lisa's mind. It was easy for a rider who was messing up a performance to just get worse. That was what Veronica had done in the dressage competition. Lisa didn't want that to happen. She wanted to get back into the competition and finish up doing her best, the way Stevie had done.

Once Pepper had cleared the third jump in the combination, Lisa used her inside leg to improve Pepper's impulsion. His back straightened out, giving more power to his hind legs. He was ready to jump again, and he was ready to jump right. Lisa finished up her performance as well as she'd started it. That was something to be proud of.

"Nice recovery!" Carole said. "You did your best and you should be proud."

"Yeah, it was great," Stevie added. She held Pepper steady while Lisa dismounted. She began walking him to cool him down. "Now, we have a little break until the awards and parade this afternoon. Let's find someplace quiet to talk, okay?"

Both Lisa and Carole thought that was a good idea. Stevie led Pepper through the stable to his stall. On her way, she saw a garbage bin and recalled the gum wrapper in her pocket. She paused and fished it out.

"Can't believe what pigs some people are," she said, tossing the wrapper into the bin.

"Oh, right," Carole agreed. She stuck her hand into her own pocket and fished out the gum wrapper she'd picked up the day before in the woods. "And watermelon bubble gum at that. Yuck!"

"Watermelon?" Stevie said, peering into the trash bin, looking for the wrapper she'd just tossed there. "That was the flavor of the one I picked up, too."

"In the woods?" Carole asked.

"No," Stevie said. "It was by the telephone . . ." Stevie suddenly got the feeling of a lot of odd facts coming together, and sticking together, like *bubble gum!*

"Put your horses in the stalls and just loosen their girths. Make it quick, too," she said. "We'll meet in the hayloft in five minutes, flat!"

Stevie disappeared too fast for her friends to ask any questions. Carole and Lisa decided to disappear just as fast. All their questions would be answered in the loft.

"EVERY TIME I look at all these pieces, I keep coming up with one name," Stevie began. "And that name is Donald." She told them about the phone call she'd overheard earlier. "At first, I didn't think anything about it. But when I did think, I thought about gum wrappers and bubble gum. Everything here seems to be held together by gum wrappers and bubble gum."

"Including ransom notes!" Carole said.

"Precisely," Stevie agreed.

"Do you really think Donald is a horsenapper?" Lisa asked. It seemed impossible that somebody who was so industrious and hard-working could also be a crook.

"I don't know," Stevie admitted. "I am pretty sure that

he's involved. The way he talked on the phone—and he *has* to be the person I heard on the phone—it sounded like somebody else was in charge and he just needed the money."

Carole scratched her head. "So, if we conclude that Donald's the errand boy for the crooks, where does that put the horses?"

"In the woods, of course," Stevie said.

"But they weren't at the quarry. What makes you so sure they're in the woods at all?"

"The gum wrapper," Stevie said. "Plus the fact that Donald was riding around those woods. I don't think he actually followed us there. I think he was there already and just heard us. That's when he made up the story about following us."

"So where are the horses?" Carole asked. "And how did they get there without the van?"

"I don't know," Stevie admitted. "But we're just going to have to go look. And this time, we'll find them."

"I think it's time to tighten Pepper's girth again," Lisa said, standing up. "And on the way, I'll check to make sure Donald is very busy doing something that will occupy him for a long time."

They agreed to meet at the good-luck horseshoe in five minutes.

SEVERAL THINGS MADE The Saddle Club feel they needed to hurry. In Carole's mind, it was that every minute the horses were captured, they were endangered. As far as Stevie was concerned, she wanted to rush so she and her friends would be the first ones to find, and free, the horses. Lisa's main concern was that the mystery be unraveled before most people knew there was a mystery—and that the girls hadn't told anyone about it.

Each of them knew this about one another as they rode quickly along the fire road that morning, and each found it comforting. It was as if they'd divvied up what had to be worried about and thus had everything covered. At least they *hoped* it was everything.

Once again, they followed the rutted path to the left when it forked. Carole reasoned that Stevie's theory was still good. The ruts *could* have been a horse van and everything seemed undisturbed on the right-hand fork. Once again, when they came to the creek, they were puzzled. The tire tracks not only stopped there, but seemed to turn around.

"So, now what do we do?" Stevie asked.

Carole thought. As she did that, Starlight leaned down and began to drink the fresh water. He even took a couple of steps into the creek where he could get the faster-moving water. It reminded her of how he'd wanted to drink the water when she was on the cross-country course. And that reminded her of how much horses enjoyed being in water on a hot summer day.

"The creek!" Carole said.

"No duh," Stevie remarked sarcastically. "Sure looks like one to me."

In spite of herself, Carole laughed. "That's not what I mean," she said. "I mean I bet they took the horses out of the van—which left a trail in the mud and which couldn't go any farther than this—and walked them through the creek, which left no trail at all!"

"Oh!" Lisa exclaimed. "That would explain a lot."

Stevie nodded excitedly. "It even explains why Donald was coming from upstream when he claimed he'd been following us from the other direction. Let's go!"

"Quietly," Carole added. She didn't have to say it twice. They proceeded walking upstream in the creek.

Carole didn't know the woods in this direction and it wasn't even familiar to Stevie. They were at the edge of the state forest where it bordered on some old farmland, and riders had been advised not to risk trespassing. That seemed a small crime to add to horsenapping, and Carole thought they would be forgiven.

She watched the creek bed carefully. It was shallow and the water was clear. She still wanted to be alert to any problems that might come for Starlight, Pepper, and Topside. Three horses were already in peril. She didn't want to make it six. And then she saw something that made her heart skip a beat.

"Look!" she signaled to her friends. "Manure!"

They all drew to a halt and looked. There, plain as anything, was a pile of manure.

"I never thought I'd see the day when manure looked good to me!" Stevie joked.

"Where there's manure, there are horses!" Lisa declared. "Right now, I think I like that even better than the one about smoke and fire."

"Somehow I doubt it'll catch on like the smoke-and-fire saying," Stevie joked.

Carole felt irrationally elated by the presence of manure on the bank of the creek. It certainly was evidence that they were on the right trail. But what lay around the next bend? How close were they? How much danger were the horses in? How much danger were *they* in?

The same thought seemed to occur to her friends then, too. The three of them sat silently, nervously, on their horses. Carole looked ahead thoughtfully. Starlight's ears perked up, as if he were thinking, too. Then, over the gurgling sound of the creek, the occasional chirrups of birds overhead, and the rustle of leaves as squirrels darted back and forth, came a more familiar, welcome sound. It was the sound of a horse's whinny.

The girls looked at one another. They all knew then that they had found what they were looking for.

"We've got to go for help," Lisa whispered.

"We've got to stay and help the horses," Carole told her.

"We've got to be absolutely positive," Stevie said sensibly.

Without further discussion, the girls dismounted and secured their horses' reins to a low branch. On foot they followed the bank of the creek around the next bend. They snuck behind a large rock and peered over the hill.

There, in a small hollow, was one of Willow Creek's isolated farms. From the look of the condition of the barn and the house, Stevie thought it might even be an abandoned farm. The buildings were still standing, but they hadn't seen the business end of a paintbrush for many, many years.

"What a dump," Lisa said disdainfully.

"Nobody's going to hide stolen horses at the Waldorf

Astoria," Stevie said. "This place looks just about perfect."

"So, where are the stolen horses?" Lisa asked.

"We'll see them in a minute," Carole said. From where they were crouched, they could see the back of the barn and the house. They couldn't see anything in either building or on the far side of either building, and they couldn't see any activity, human or equine.

"We've got to get to the edge of the barn there," Stevie said.

"One of us does," Carole corrected her. "I'll go. You two stay here. There's no point in all three of us getting into trouble."

To Stevie and Lisa, the suggestion seemed a little silly, since it was clear that all three of them were probably already in a lot of trouble, but they nevertheless stayed put while Carole crept forward toward the barn.

Carole could feel it in her bones. She was right. They were right. The horses were here, and so were the horsenappers. All they had to do was spot them and then go for help.

It only took a few seconds to cover the thirty yards to the side of the barn. There were no windows on that side. She had to creep to the front and look around the edge. She flattened herself against the wall, afraid even of casting a shadow that might be noticed.

Carole peered around the edge of the old barn and

found that her greatest hopes and worst fears were all being fulfilled at once. For there were two strange men and three familiar horses. That was the good news. The bad news was that the men were trying to load the horses onto a van. They were going to move them, and there would be no way for The Saddle Club to follow them. The horses could be lost forever!

The men were trying to load Garnet first. The one thing working to Carole's advantage, to say nothing of Garnet's, was that Garnet hated riding on vans. The only way Veronica, or really Red, because he was always the one to do it, could get her on a van was to put a blindfold on her. It wouldn't take the horsenappers long to figure that out, but it might take long enough for Carole to do what had to be done.

She had to get Lisa and Stevie there to help, plus Pepper, Starlight, and Topside, and it all had to be a surprise. She turned to her friends and waved, then pointed to their own horses. Stevie nodded. She was always eager for an adventure and she knew just what to do.

Stevie and Lisa disappeared. Carole held her breath for a few seconds until she heard the sound she most wanted to hear. It was Stevie and Lisa coming over the hill on horseback, bringing Starlight with them.

Carole knew they didn't have much time. The horse-nappers would hear the horses and know something was up. They might have the advantage of surprise, but they wouldn't have it for long.

Carole ran to meet her friends. In a second, she was in Starlight's saddle.

"It's roundup time!" she said.

She nudged Starlight hard with her calves. He responded instantly and the three girls rode around the corner of the barn into the open area by the van at the same time. Two men gaped at them in astonishment.

"What the . . . ?" one of the men said.

Carole answered his question with action. Sat and Bodoni were in a small paddock next to the van. One of the men held Garnet by a lead rope.

"Open the paddock gate," Carole called to Stevie. "I'll get Garnet."

"That's what you think!" the other man said fiercely. He challenged her by swinging at her with his fist. That was a fight Carole would lose, so it was a battle she wouldn't enter. Instead, she let Garnet do the "getting" for her. She rode up behind the mare and gave her a hard smack on the rear—not enough to hurt her, just enough to surprise her. Garnet, who hadn't liked the idea of the van, was nervous anyway. The smack on her rump was all she needed to convince her to bolt, and bolt she did, right into the woods toward the creek, just where Carole wanted her.

Carole turned to see what her friends were up to. Stevie had the gate of the paddock open. Lisa rode Pepper in and circled behind Sat and Bodoni. "Hiyaaaa!" she cried, roundup style. "Git along little dogie!" Sat and Bodoni were as surprised as Garnet had been. They fled through the gate, and when they tried to veer to the left, Carole was there to steer them toward the woods, too.

"Let's get out of here!" Stevie yelled, following the three freed horses into the woods.

"You took the words right out of my mouth!" Carole agreed. Starlight, Pepper, and Topside fled from the old farmyard as quickly as they'd entered it. The last thing Carole heard before she entered the woods after the horses was the sound of the engine on the horse van revving up.

The woods around the farmhouse were thick. There was no path there, except for the creek. The horses, perhaps because they'd been that way once before, naturally headed for the creek. That was a good thing, because The Saddle Club would have had a rough time trying to round them up out of the dense underbrush. The best part about the creek, though, was that it wasn't too wide. It wasn't, for example, wide enough for a horse van, though there was one trying to follow them into it.

Carole heard a loud noise that sounded an awful lot like metal hitting wood. It was followed by a loud outburst of words that her father told her Marines sometimes said. Carole pulled Starlight to a halt and looked over her shoulder. It was a beautiful sight. The horse van was tightly wedged between two trees at a narrow section of the creek. The horsenappers would never catch up with them now.

"Hey, we're home free!" Stevie announced joyously.

"As long as we can get the horses back to Pine Hollow safely," Carole said.

"In time to call the police so they can get back to the farm and arrest those guys before they skedaddle," Lisa finished.

That was true. Sooner or later, the horsenappers would be able to back out of the creek, and as soon as that happened, they'd be gone.

"Let's go!" Stevie said, urging her friends, though it wasn't necessary. They were all moving their horses as fast as possible.

The girls had spent some time on a dude ranch in the Southwest with a friend of theirs named Kate Devine. They'd been on a genuine cattle roundup and had learned some skills that they put to use. They knew they had to surround the herd as well as they could, even if it was only a herd of three.

Carole went first. She picked up the lead rope tied to Garnet's halter and began riding forward down the creek. Lisa was in the rear. It was her job to see to it that the other two horses kept up with the group. Stevie had the trickiest job. She rode in the center and she had to see that Sat and Bodoni stayed in line. As long as they were riding in the creek bed, it wasn't hard, but as soon as they reached the fire road, where the woods opened up considerably, it became trickier.

Bodoni was not only a beautiful black stallion, he was also bold and independent. He seemed to get an idea in his head about showing off for the two mares, Garnet and Sat, and that made Stevie's job much harder. She had to pay a lot more attention to Bodoni than to the horse she was riding. Fortunately, Topside was good at doing what he was told, even when his rider wasn't paying all that much attention to him.

This was where Stevie's dressage training stood her in good stead. They weren't riding for ribbons, they were riding for real. Every time Bodoni veered off to the right, Topside circled around behind him and headed him back to the left. Sat, it seemed, was tired and was perfectly satisfied to simply follow Carole and Garnet. She didn't cause Stevie any trouble at all, though she did drop behind a few times to nibble at the grass. Lisa tugged at her mane once and used her riding crop on her flank occasionally to remind her that her job was to move forward. She willingly followed along.

Although it had seemed like a world of time, because so much had happened, when Carole looked at her watch she saw that she and Stevie and Lisa had only been gone from Pine Hollow for two hours. Now, as they emerged from the woods and Pine Hollow was only a couple of hundred yards away, all of them felt the same relief and eagerness to return. That was especially true of Bodoni. It was as if he could smell the hay and oats he knew he'd get. That was enough to make him pick up his pace. Before Stevie and Topside could do anything about it, Bodoni was cantering, and then *galloping* toward Pine Hollow.

There was nothing for the girls to do but gallop with him. They followed along the street by Pine Hollow, and when Bodoni crossed, they crossed, too. Fortunately, there was no traffic coming at all.

Bodoni didn't stop at Pine Hollow's stable, he proceeded right past it, through the parking area, around the barriers, past the spectator stands, and right smack into the ring where the stadium jumping was taking place. One astonished rider, in the middle of the adult competition jump course, drew her horse to a halt and demanded to know, "What's going on here?" A lot more people asked the same question when Carole, Lisa, and Stevie, on Starlight, Pepper, and Topside, arrived along with Garnet and Sat. Starlight was so hyped by the invigorating gallop that he even jumped one of the fences on the jump course. Carole tried not to smile. She didn't succeed.

At that point, Max Regnery ran into the ring. His face

was red with anger. "I'm sure there's some explanation for this!" he blurted out furiously.

Stevie drew Topside to a halt in front of him. A big grin crossed her face. "You bet there is!" she announced proudly.

IT TOOK A few minutes to round up Bodoni and get him safely into a stall. Garnet and Sat were tired out and only too willing to be led to safety by Carole, who put them in stalls and gave them fresh water and clean hay. It took a few more minutes for Stevie to explain some of what had been going on to Max.

While these things were happening, Lisa had another job to do. She called the police. It took more than a little effort to convince them that she knew what she was talking about and they didn't have any time to waste. Finally, she told them that if they missed out on the collar of the century just because they didn't believe her, they would look pretty silly. The dispatcher said a car would go to the farm immediately—and one would come to Pine Hollow to talk to her as well.

"Good," she said. "There's somebody here they have to meet, too."

When she hung up the phone, Lisa found herself laughing out loud. She'd astonished herself by using the expression "collar of the century." That was the sort of thing *Stevie* would say, not the kind of thing straight-A-student Lisa would say. She decided to thank Stevie for the inspiration.

"You what?" Max asked, astonished, as Stevie finished telling the story of their rescue.

Stevie just nodded. There was no point in telling it again. He'd heard it right. She told him as much.

"You rounded them up and herded them away from the—what did you call them—*horsenappers*? But how did you know?"

There was a good question. Stevie had known from the beginning that they really ought to have told at least Max what was going on. There was no way they should have taken the chances they did, but they'd taken them for good reasons. If they had told, all of the horses would have been endangered and maybe none of them ever would have made it back. Still, if Stevie let on that they had actually seen the ransom note, they could be in more hot water than even she was willing to risk. So Max's question hung in the air. *How did you know?*

Then inspiration struck. "Elementary, my dear Regnery," she said. "Elementary."

The answer was so astonishing that Max forgot that he hadn't learned anything from it. He just burst into laughter and so did all the other people standing around.

A FEW MINUTES later a police car pulled into Pine Hollow. Lisa met the officers at the front door and brought them around to the back, where the combined-training event had been taking place until it was interrupted by the arrival of the rescued horses. Lisa wanted the police to talk to Stevie. She was the best at explaining what had happened. It took a while to unravel the whole story, but Stevie managed it, without mentioning the "missing" ransom note. She just said that their suspicions were aroused when all the expensive purebred horses seemed to be mysteriously withdrawing and disappearing. The part she had the hardest time explaining was the significance of the bubble-gum wrappers. The police just kept exchanging confused looks.

"Oh, forget about how we figured out what was going on," she said. "We just did. And then, we trailed the horses into the woods . . ."

"So, where is this gum chewer?" one of the officers asked.

"I don't know," Stevie said. "Carole, what did you do with him?"

"Oh, you'll find him in the tack room," Carole said with a mischievous grin on her face. "I told him Mrs. Reg wanted him to polish the dressage saddles. All of them. You may find him reluctant to leave. He's a very hard worker!"

Everybody who had seen Donald dashing around and working extremely hard, just to cover up the fact that he was doing things he shouldn't have been doing, laughed. He *was* a hard worker.

The police emerged from the tack room a few minutes later, bringing Donald with them. They explained that they would be taking him back to the station house as soon as their colleagues returned from fetching the horsenappers from the van in the woods.

"I think we have some time, then," Max said. "Why don't we finish up the event?" Then he turned to his mother. "And while we're watching the last two riders, could you call the owners of the three rescued horses and tell them what a wonderful show some of our junior riders have put on today?"

"I'd be pleased to," Mrs. Reg said. "It seems small thanks since, after all, because of them, all the dressage saddles are clean as whistles!"

It was just like Mrs. Reg to think of the tack at a time like that.

The one disappointment Stevie, Lisa, and Carole had was that they had missed almost all of the adult jumping competition. Max saw to it that they got front-row seats to watch the final competitors. The adult course had more obstacles in it and they were higher, but the rules were the same. It was fun and exciting to watch the competitors, but, they all agreed, it had been more fun competing themselves.

When the last jump was cleared and the final salute given, Max announced that the parade and ribbon ceremony would begin in fifteen minutes. That allowed Red and a few volunteers enough time to take down the jumps and it allowed riders who hadn't competed in the advanced competition enough time to saddle their horses.

Carole though Starlight looked less than enthusiastic about the idea of donning his saddle another time that day. "This is the last time," she promised him. "And it's going to be easy. No wild rides through the woods, no tracking through water, no jumps. Just a nice walk around the show ring and then a few times up and back to the judges for ribbons, okay?" He still seemed skeptical, but Carole thought he'd change his mind when he had a ribbon clipped to his bridle. She gave him a carrot in the meantime and that seemed to help, too.

All of the riders lined up as they had practiced before the event for the final parade. Mrs. Reg put some marching music on the public-address system and they all rode into the ring. It reminded The Saddle Club of the rodeo parade they'd been in once. The crowd, stirred up by the excitement of the rescue of the horses, stood and cheered for all of the riders as they entered. Carole felt exhilarated. She had always known that she would enjoy competing, but she'd never known it would be as exciting as this. She simply loved it, especially knowing that she and Starlight had done their best, both in the event and in the rescue operation. She hoped she'd never have to save a horsenap victim again, but she also hoped it wouldn't be long before she was in another horse show.

The riders all drew to a halt, and turned to stand in a row, facing the judges' stand.

There were a lot of awards to give out. Each event had first- through sixth-place winners, junior and senior.

When Max began handing out ribbons, Carole thought it seemed like it was just The Saddle Club show. In junior dressage, Stevie took the blue ribbon for first place, Lisa got red for second place, and Carole took a yellow for third place. Carole thought she was pretty lucky to have gotten third, but Stevie certainly deserved first and Lisa was just right in second place.

Then, for cross-country, Lisa got the blue ribbon. She was the only rider of all the junior entrants to have had a "clear" round without any mistakes, within the time limit. Stevie and Carole clapped long and loud for her. She'd worked hard on her riding skills and deserved that blue ribbon. Carole got second place, which surprised her, and Stevie took third. Then came the jumping awards and it still seemed like The Saddle Club show. Carole was the undisputed winner, and everybody who had seen her perform stood up again to give her and Starlight one more round of applause. Stevie got second place in that and Lisa took third.

"Doesn't anybody else ever win anything?" Stevie whispered to Carole. Carole knew Stevie was joking. After all, Max was giving lots of ribbons to other people. It's just that he was giving all the best ones to Carole and her friends. And, she decided, that was okay because they deserved them!

Then Max gave out the awards to the adult riders. There had been a lot of competitors in the adult division and there were a lot of ribbons to hand out. Carole didn't mind waiting through that, though. After all, she was doing something she loved. It wasn't just that she was in the saddle of her very own horse, though that was important. Nor was it that they were standing in the middle of a show ring, surrounded by an audience that had only recently spent a fair amount of time clapping for them, though that was nice, too. The best part was that when Carole looked straight forward, as she was supposed to, aiming her eyes between her horse's ears, he had three well-deserved ribbons flapping from his bridle!

"And that brings us to the conclusion of our awards ceremony," Max told the audience. "Except for two very special awards. In each division, we award a 'Blue ribbon' to the rider who accumulated fewer penalty points than all the others in each of the three categories. In the adult division, this is an easy matter because the winner is clearly John Malcolm." He handed Mr. Malcolm his ribbon and there was polite applause.

"In the junior division, however, it's not an easy matter, as those of you who were paying attention will realize." He paused.

Carole, Lisa, and Stevie all looked at one another. They hadn't even known that there was such a thing as the "Best in Show" ribbon. It had been enough that each of them had excelled in one of the three events. That had made it easy to root for each other. *But,* Stevie thought, *if there was an overall ribbon for the single best rider . . .*

"As you can see, we have three girls here who have done almost equally exceptionally well, finishing one-two-three in all three events."

It would have to go to . . .

"So, choosing one from among them is almost impossible, but it's a task I took on when I organized this event. So, I'm pleased to announce—"

Lisa leaned over to Carole. "It's got to be you, Carole."

Carole, Stevie said to herself.

"—Carole Hanson is hereby awarded the 'Best in Show'!"

"Me?" Carole said, gasping with surprise.

"Of course," her friends said in a single voice.

"Come on over here, Carole. Take your ribbon and enjoy a victory gallop along with Mr. Malcolm."

A few minutes later, Carole decided that the only thing prettier than three ribbons hanging off of Starlight's bridle was four ribbons flapping gaily as she galloped around the ring.

13

THREE MORE POLICE cars had arrived by the time the members of The Saddle Club were ready to untack their horses for the final time that day.

Mrs. Reg told the girls that the police wanted to see them.

"I bet they do," Lisa said darkly. "They want to slap cuffs on us and put us in the pokey right next to the horsenappers."

"Or *instead* of the horsenappers!" Stevie suggested.

"No way," Carole said. "This is the day we all get blue ribbons in everything, including crime prevention. We can go see them as soon as we're finished up, but first, our horses deserve a good grooming and feeding. We owe them some thanks, you know."

Lisa and Stevie agreed. However, they didn't think

that necessarily meant they had to take a long time at the grooming. Within fifteen minutes, the three girls met up with the policeman who was waiting for them in the tack room.

Mrs. Reg introduced him as Officer Kent. He was a big man who looked very severe and frightening in his uniform. Even Carole, who was quite accustomed to uniforms, found herself a little intimidated. All thoughts about blue ribbons in everything fled from her mind as she listened to the man's serious voice. "We found two men trapped in a van stuck between two trees," he began. "That's just about what one of you described on the phone. We've talked to a young man here, named Donald, and he told us a story pretty much like the one we heard that another one of you told Mr. Regnery about horsenapping and ransom."

He paused. "Now, we've spoken with the owners of Saturday's Child and Bodoni. It seems they got ransom notes and decided not to tell us about it because they were afraid for their horses. We've also reached a Miss Veronica diAngelo, a friend of yours?"

"Not exactly—" Stevie began.

Carole didn't think there was any need to tell the officer what a pain Veronica was. She gave Stevie a nudge and said "Yes."

Officer Kent observed the nudge. It seemed significant to him. "Well, she won't tell us a thing. She denies knowing anything about it. I know how you girls are, though. I'm sure you're just covering up for one another." He paused again. Carole realized he was waiting for somebody to confirm his suspicion, but the idea was so bizarre that all he got were astonished looks from the three of them. He read those looks as the confirmation he'd wanted. "Ah, I can tell by the looks on your faces that I've hit home. I know you won't reveal the whole truth, but it's clear that you all felt sorry for Veronica when she told you that her horse was kidnapped and you decided to take matters into your own hands."

Carole was tempted to tell him that it wasn't *Veronica* they felt sorry for, but she kept her mouth closed.

He went on then for a while, telling them how even experienced and trained police officers could get into difficulty when they were dealing with unfamiliar situations, and young girls should never attempt . . .

Carole knew he was right, in a way, and she wanted to tell him what had really happened, but as she listened, it became apparent that Officer Kent was coming up with a perfect explanation for everything they'd done wrong. Why should she help him out and get herself and her friends in loads of trouble?

"Anyway," he continued. "It's clear to me that this has all worked out for the best and I'm not one to stir things up when the ending is fine. You three will no doubt receive a lot of attention in the next few days. Enjoy it, but don't let it go to your heads. I don't ever want you solving another mystery for my department again. Understood?"

Lisa and Stevie nodded. Carole saluted. It was an automatic reaction for a Marine Corps colonel's daughter. She couldn't help herself. The officer saluted back.

When Officer Kent and The Saddle Club emerged from the tack room, the girls were astonished at the crowd that had gathered. First of all, all their parents were there. They practically smothered their daughters with hugs. Even Stevie's brothers hugged her.

"I never thought of you as a hero before," her little brother, Michael, said.

"It's just in the genes," her twin brother, Alex, claimed. Stevie gave him a withering look.

Alicia and Mr. Feeney were there. They both came and hugged the girls and thanked them for saving their horses.

"Oh, Carole, I'm so sorry I was mean to you," Alicia said.

"I know," Carole said. "You were just scared. I don't blame you. If I'd had any sense, I'd have been scared, too."

"Maybe," Alicia agreed. "But in that case, I'm glad you didn't have any sense! If you had, where would Bodoni be today?"

That was a question Carole decided she and her

friends would have to think about long and hard. She wanted to talk to them. She felt the real need for a Saddle Club meeting, but there was a mass of people, all of whom seemed to want to talk to the three girls together. There was no way they could get away, at least for a while.

Then, a silence fell on the crowd as a Mercedes-Benz drew into the drive at Pine Hollow. The doors opened and out stepped Mr. and Mrs. diAngelo, obviously just returned from their trip because they were both still wearing dressy clothes, and Veronica. She was wearing a pout.

Mr. diAngelo set the example for his wife and daughter. He went to Stevie first because she was the closest to him.

"I think we owe you all our sincerest thanks," he said, offering his hand.

"We were glad to help Garnet," Stevie said pointedly.

"She's a beautiful horse," Carole said. "We couldn't let her be stolen."

"Well, you saved me an awful lot of money," Mr. diAngelo said. "I heard those men wanted ten thousand dollars to give her back. I'm grateful to you. All of you," he said then, reaching for Lisa's hand. "And I'm sure my wife and daughter want to thank you, too."

Mrs. diAngelo stepped forward and reached out as far as she could, as if she didn't want to get too close to the likes of Stevie, Lisa, and Carole. She shook each of their hands by the fingertips in turn and nodded, acknowledging the good work the girls had done.

Then it was Veronica's turn. She came up closer than her mother had—so close that only the girls could hear her. "I didn't want her back, you know," she said. "That darned horse cost me a blue ribbon. I think I'm going to have Daddy sell her and see if he can buy me a good horse, maybe Topside. I bet Max would sell him to me."

"In August," Stevie agreed. "When it snows." She nodded and smiled sweetly. "And you're welcome, Veronica."

Veronica glared at her. Then she stepped back so her glare included all three of The Saddle Club members.

"I'm exhausted with worry, Mother," she said. "I must go home now."

"Yes, dear," she said. "Here, take my arm."

"I think I'm going to throw up," Stevie whispered to Carole.

"Not on the Mercedes!" Carole said in mock horror.

Veronica and her mother disappeared into the car, behind its darkened windows.

Mr. diAngelo seemed decidedly uncomfortable, even embarrassed, by the performance of his wife and his daughter.

"They're just so upset," he began.

"We understand," Lisa said. "The whole thing has been upsetting to everyone."

He nodded, apparently relieved that he didn't have to apologize any more. "Anyway, I wanted you girls to know that I am truly grateful. Veronica is blaming Garnet for her own failure. Surely you know that. She's feeling bitter, but she'll get over it. While she was thinking only of herself, you three did something quite wonderful for her and for two other people, and you will be rewarded. I am going to give you five hundred dollars, which is small thanks for what you did for us."

Three jaws dropped at once.

"No," Carole protested. "We didn't—"

"Yes," Mr. diAngelo said. He disappeared into the car then, too, and closed his door, silently, to end the discussion.

The car pulled out of the Pine Hollow driveway. The police had left by then and the reporter dashed off, saying something about word processors and deadlines. The three girls were left alone.

"Don't just stand there," Max said from behind them. "There's work to do. We've got two horses boarding here overnight that weren't supposed to be here, and we're shorthanded because it seems that one of our stablehands got his hand into something that wasn't so stable, so he's going to be explaining a few things to the police. Do you think you three girls could pitch in, for once, and help us around here?"

Being in the limelight was nice, but it was nice when things were back to normal, too.

"You mean we can groom Sat and Bodoni?" Carole asked.

"I don't know who else is going to do it," Max said. "Garnet, too. I think those three need extraspecial grooming today and I can't think of anybody who deserves the honor more than the three of you."

"I get Garnet!" Lisa said.

"I'll take Bodoni," Carole offered.

"I'm satisfied with Sat," Stevie said. "And when we're done with this, how about a little trip to TD's? I think we have a few things to talk about . . ."

"More than a few," Carole agreed.

ONCE AGAIN, THE trio was in their favorite booth. This time, TD's was even better than it had been the last time they'd been there, since there seemed to be almost no possibility that one Veronica diAngelo would come in to show off a new pair of garnet earrings.

"Five hundred dollars!" Stevie said. "Think of it. Think of all the wonderful things we could do with that kind of money!"

Carole shook her head. "We can't take that money from him," she said. "No way. It would mean that we did what we did because of money. We didn't. We just did that because the horses were in danger."

"We did it because it was fun, too," Stevie reminded her. "Actually, it was so much fun, I think we should go into the business. There probably won't be a lot of horsenapping around here in the near future—our reputation will keep them out of the county, you know—but we can solve other kinds of mysteries. We can, sort of, like, open up shop."

"Your idea of fun isn't exactly always *my* idea of fun," Lisa said sensibly. "You heard what Officer Kent said, didn't you? We could have been in real trouble. We could have gotten the horses hurt *and* we could have gotten ourselves hurt. Remember how we felt when we thought they'd kidnapped Veronica?"

It was a sobering thought. "Yes, I do," Stevie said. "And I remember how disappointed I felt when we found out that they hadn't!"

The girls giggled. It was true. Veronica was being so poisonous that they had wished, just a little bit, that somebody might have found a way to teach her a lesson.

"Oh," Stevie said, suddenly quiet, but with a smile on her face.

"What's the 'oh' for?" Carole asked.

"I've got it," she said.

"What?" Lisa asked.

"I've just figured out exactly why we have to keep the five hundred dollars Mr. diAngelo wants to pay us."

"I'm telling you, it's not right," Carole said.

"Why?" Lisa asked Stevie.

"Because it will make Veronica diAngelo absolutely, totally, completely, and outrageously furious."

"Oh!" Lisa said.

Stevie looked at Carole. She nodded. "Yes," she agreed. "You are absolutely, totally, completely, and outrageously right. We'll keep the money. We'll just have to be careful about how we're going to spend it."

"I know how I'm going to spend the first couple of dollars," Lisa said, seeing that the waitress was on her way to their table. "I'm going to have hot caramel on vanilla ice cream." The waitress jotted it down. She looked at Carole.

"I'll have hot fudge on mint chip."

The waitress wrote that down. Then she turned to Stevie. "Vanilla?" she asked hopefully.

"No way," Stevie said. "I want, um, raspberry swirl with pineapple chunks and chocolate sauce, covered with whipped cream."

The woman gaped.

"Oh, and don't forget the cherry on top, will you?" The waitress fled to the kitchen.

Things were back to normal for The Saddle Club, and that was just absolutely, totally, completely, and outrageously fine with all of them.

ABOUT THE AUTHOR

BONNIE BRYANT is the author of more than forty books for young readers, including novelizations of movie hits such as *Teenage Mutant Ninja Turtles* and *Honey, I Shrunk the Kids*, written under her married name, B. B. Hiller.

Ms. Bryant began writing The Saddle Club in 1986. Although she had done some riding before that, she intensified her studies then and found herself learning right along with her characters Stevie, Carole, and Lisa. She claims that they are all much better riders than she is.

Ms. Bryant was born and raised in New York City. Her husband and sometime coauthor, Neil Hiller, died in 1989. She lives in Greenwich Village with her two sons.

We hope you enjoyed reading this book. If you would like to receive further information about available titles in the Bantam series, just write to the address below, with your name and address: Kim Prior, Bantam Books, 61–63 Uxbridge Road, Ealing, London W5 5SA.

If you live in Australia or New Zealand and would like more information about the series, please write to:

Sally Porter
Transworld Publishers
(Australia) Pty Ltd
15–25 Helles Avenue
Moorebank
NSW 2170
AUSTRALIA

Kiri Martin
Transworld Publishers (NZ) Ltd
3 William Pickering Drive
Albany
Auckland
NEW ZEALAND

All Bantam and Young Adult books are available at your bookshop or newsagent, or can be ordered from the following address:
Corgi/Bantam Books, Cash Sales Department, PO Box 11, Falmouth, Cornwall, TR10 9EN.

Please list the title(s) you would like, and send together with a cheque or postal order to cover the cost of the book(s) plus postage and packing charges of £1.00 for one book, £1.50 for two books, and an additional 30p for each subsequent book ordered to a maximum of £3.00 for seven or more books.

(The above applies only to readers in the UK, and BFPO)

Overseas customers (including Eire), please allow £2.00 for postage and packing for the first book, an additional £1.00 for a second book, and 50p for each subsequent title ordered.

SWEET VALLEY TWINS

Follow the adventures of Jessica, Elizabeth and all their friends at Sweet Valley as twelve-year-olds. A super series with one new title every month!